Sister Myrtle

Ebony Jasper Eldritch

Table of Contents

A Foreword by Sister Eleanor Jesse

My name is Sister Eleanor Jesse, a nun and former investigator of supernatural events for the Catholic Church.

I have, put bluntly, had a very long and... interesting... life, one dedicated to helping others by any means I can – a life of fighting sin and evil.

As I sit here, writing this, it is the morning of 31st May, in the year 2021, and I am ninety-seven. I was born 17th April 1924 in Liverpool, a grimy, impoverished and rather drab city back then. Because of this, my parents sent me away at the age of fourteen just before the Second World War began, to a convent in the country somewhere, I forget now the details of it. They started training me up as a nun there, and after both my parents passed away in the war – my father abroad, blown to bits by artillery in the trenches, and my mother by starvation as she was overtaken by poverty – I, being an only child, felt the only meaning left in my life was the Church, and threw myself into my studies wholeheartedly.

I took my vows when I was twenty, in 1945, and managed to get a position as an investigator of the supernatural under the great Father Martin Vivicelli in 1949. It is not common knowledge I think that the Vatican has a number of investigators of the supernatural in their employ. Exorcists are, truth be told, the most famous among this little brood, and certainly have the greatest skills. Father Martin was a wonderfully skilled Exorcist and if it weren't for him certainly a good few hundred people would have tragically lost their lives and their souls to the sinful hands of Hell's dark forces.

I was Father Martin's final apprentice before he passed away in 1952, and on many occasions did he tell me I had always been his favourite. I do not know how many investigators he tutored before me, but I know it was a great number.

In 1951, seventy years ago now, I finally was brought up past the rank of apprentice and I was given my very first case as a fully-fledged investigator of supernatural events, my first case being in the winter at the dawn of 1951. I was twenty-six years of age then, practically a baby! In those days I had keener wits than now, and certainly I was no fool, but I confess my wisdom was lacking certainly.

I had, by that time, spent twelve years in the Church, being a nun for half that time and an apprentice investigator for the last two years, but none of that stood a chance of preparing me for what was ahead.

Looking back at it now, however, I had already learned everything I could learn from a book or a teacher or a class, it was experience and wisdom I now had to gain, and the only way to gain those things is to get out there into the world and do them. Father Martin had taken me out there plenty of times, but never was I alone at the forefront of it all, and I confess that though I certainly thought I knew everything... well there's an art to that job. You can know it all and still be useless because wisdom and experience come not just from the mind but from the heart and the soul.

My mind was ready.

And on this first case, I finally found out after all that time whether my heart could take it too.

I, of course, survived, but that doesn't mean what I went through was easy!

I was encouraged to begin writing this story a few years ago by an old friend of mine, one Professor Jules Agincourt, a man who deals with many of the same sorts of affairs as I do, though he specialises in the bestial while I excel in more spiritual matters. Jules knows well I have a great many stories to tell, indeed I believe I have worked some eight or nine hundred cases throughout my career.

I have been retired since 2007 and I have spent the last fourteen years trying desperately hard to forget the grotesque details of my career, but alas I find myself often unable to stop the nightmares.

Perhaps this will help.

I am, as I said, three years away from being a century old and I doubt greatly that I will live long enough to be able to tell all of my stories, but here and now I can make a start. Here and now, I can tell you the tale of my first case, the case of St. Agnes Convent near Ashton in Inverness, of Sister Myrtle, and of Kazzkhan.

I will warn you now, this is not a pleasant tale. Read on at your own risk!

The things contained herein are real. The people I speak of were once real people who lived and have – most likely of old age by now – died.

The dark forces are real.

The words I spoke were real.

The things I saw, the things I fought... they were real.

This might make you uncomfortable, it might make you feel sick and it will almost certainly scare your pants off.

Even now, I still have nightmares. Those things I saw... those people and what they were suffering through...

It still gives me nightmares, even now, even after seventy years.

So be ready...

Chapter 1: The Facts Before The Inquiry

In January of 1951, I was assigned my first case as an investigator of supernatural events for the Vatican. My supervisor, Father Martin Vivicelli, was the one to deliver the news to me, though on that day I think he wished he could be anywhere else in the world.

Father Martin was at that time some eighty years old, an age which at the time had made him seem to me as a withered husk, barely held together. Indeed, in my youth I had considered him to be of such frailty that a strong breeze might risk disintegrating his body and dispersing the dust into the atmosphere. Despite his age, he had a full head of hair that still was dark – though I confess it was dark *grey* – giving him a brooding sort of look which matched well with his dark, deep, soulful brown eyes. His face was hard-edged with deep lines and wrinkles from decades of weary frowning and as long as I'd known him his voice had been hollow and ragged after so many years of shouting exorcism rites at dark forces.

He hunched over somewhat in his old age, the frailty of his body exacerbated by time and his weariness seeming to weigh him down, bending him over into a crooked sort of figure. He was a great Exorcist and had in his tenure at the Vatican trained up too many apprentices to count, each of whom had gone on to be great and inspirational Exorcists and investigators themselves, a cohort which I was about to join, I hoped.

I was called to the Father's rooms around noon on the 8th January, and I shall never forget the weary look of brokenness upon his face when I entered the room, as though he were about to give some terrible news.

I am ninety-seven now, and a few years ago, my cat Cecil had to be put down because of some sort of cancer in his liver that he wasn't going to get better from. As I sat in that vet's office and that young man told me the terrible news of what was to become of my beloved pet and best friend, I couldn't help but recall the look Father Martin gave me that day.

It was the same look, upon the faces of the vet and my mentor, the look of terrible, tragic news, news of heartbreak; news of death.

Father Martin had been about to give me a death sentence. He was, of course, a priest, and thus sworn to a sacred vow of celibacy and therefore childlessness, but on many occasions he had told me that he rather saw me as a sort of daughter, and I confessed that, since I had lost my own father to the war, he had rather become a paternal figure in my life too.

Thus, as I came into those chambers in the Vatican, I looked upon the face of a man who knew he was about to send his daughter – or the closest thing he had to one – to her death, and that there was not a single thing he could do about it, no matter how much he wanted there to be.

"Please, take a seat," Father Martin encouraged me, gesturing to a plain wooden chair across from him over an ornate oak wooden desk.

The office was, as all things in the Vatican are, a grand affair with a white marble floor and grand, intricately detailed bookshelves lined with black leatherbound tomes and litanies of ancient wisdom. Three enormous, tall windows filled the back wall of the office and looked out into the beautiful nation at the heart of the Catholic faith, and beyond it, the skyline of Rome.

I did as instructed, sitting down, and frowned with worry rather as I prepared myself to listen to whatever dark news my mentor and closest friend was about to give me.

"The Vatican is offering you a case. You are being sent out to investigate the potential desecration of a convent near Inverness in Scotland. This marks your promotion to the rank of investigator of supernatural occurrences," Father Martin told me darkly.

I could not understand his dour demeanour. I myself was ecstatic. After all my training, this was what I had always wanted! My first case being sent off alone, this was exactly what I had been preparing for all my life, quite literally. Finally, my dreams were coming true and yet... my mentor, my best friend, my father figure... he seemed not excited but disappointed... heartbroken even.

"Is that not good?" I asked him incredulously.

10

"It is more or less a death sentence! They are sending you out there as cannon fodder but what can we do? Nothing!" Father Martin protested, a tear or two spilling from each eye.

Though we conversed in English, Father Martin Vivicelli was, as his name might suggest, an Italian man and in his frustration his accent seemed only to grow more powerful.

"I don't understand," I confessed in my confusions, rather befuddled.

"St. Agnes Convent in Inverness was destroyed four years ago nearly, in 1947. The nuns that survived there... they said terrible things had happened. They gave statements and testimonies, they told the Vatican that something evil had been found. In the last four years, seven priests have been sent to that place. Seven highly trained Exorcists have gone down there, my friends and my peers and not one of them has come back, not one! I think they would send me down there if they were not so afraid to lose me! Seven priests like me, seven great Exorcists, they have gone to Inverness and they have never come back! Now our superiors, they send you, and I know I shall lose you," Father Martin explained to me, at some moments falling away into Italian exclamations as he found English an insufficient language to express the passion of his frustrations.

I sat with him in silence for a moment, my mind racing with thoughts and feelings. I was excited to finally be sent on a case but now I felt only angry, tricked even, that our superiors had let me spend so much time and effort preparing for my first case, only to send me off on a suicide mission simply because they were tired of losing priests! I was furious, and yet now I felt more determined than ever to go!

In the foolish arrogance of my youth, I sat there in my mentor's chambers and, without reason or proof or a scintilla of evidence, I was certain that I would succeed where seven trained Exorcists with decades of experience under each of their belts had failed.

I was a fool indeed, but in those days I was still very much a young nun. My faith in God came from books and facts, not experiences and beliefs. I knew the scripture well but my devotion was to the Church and to people, not to God. Indeed that has changed since, but in those days that was who I was. A good woman, I hope, and one devoted to helping others, but in the name of God and not necessarily in the spirit of him.

I knew the facts of it all, but I had no experience in the real world, not that my shortcomings kept my arrogance at bay.

"We have no choice in the matter, do we?" I asked, filling up the sombre silence which had ebbed into the atmosphere. My mentor shook his head sadly.

"Then there is no point in debating it. I am going to Inverness and neither of us have a say in the matter any longer. So, you might as well tell me everything you can," I encouraged him.

Father Martin met my eye and I think then we understood one another well. I saw his brokenness and his pain at the thought of losing me, and he saw my frustrations and the arrogance that still fuelled me. My arrogance gave me confidence, but I think now that it only hurt his.

"Very well," he sighed eventually. "Then let us begin."

He shuffled forwards in his seat and opened a draw, pulling out a great stack of files and folders all knotted together with twine, and dumped them heftily upon the desk with a disconcerting *thud*. Father Martin began to unwind the twine and passed me the topmost file to peruse.

"St. Agnes Convent has stood in Inverness for almost four hundred years now, or did stand for almost four hundred years. As I said, it was destroyed in 1947, some kind of explosion which caused a fire. One of the sisters there, Sister Myrtle, she had something of a fascination with science and forensics apparently. She had a laboratory and the initial police report said that though they were unable to confirm anything, the fire began in her laboratory and most likely was caused by some sort of error during one of her chemical experiments," Father Martin explained to me, sneering a little at the mention of science and chemistry. It was no small secret that many members of the

12

Church rather looked down upon science, my mentor being one of them, and though it was something on which we disagreed, it was not something we found ourselves arguing about, not truly. "There were twenty-seven nuns in the convent when it burned down, only two escaped; Sister Bathsheba and Sister Clementina. The accounts they gave were... unsettling. All of this is in these files, I recommend you read them on your way to Scotland. The Church has already made your travel arrangements."

Father Martin passed me a collection of train tickets and other assorted travel documents.

I was to leave at 5pm that day, it seemed.

"Ellie, there is something terrible in that place," my mentor told me with ominous gravity. "I told you already, seven priests have gone to that place. Seven Exorcists. None of them have ever been seen again. Not one. They are all gone. It's not that I don't believe in you, but this *is* a suicide mission. I have faith in you. Please be smart, please be reasonable, please come back in one piece. The Church has no idea where their priests keep disappearing to, that's why they keep sending more. It's why they're sending you. They would stop sending people, but... well, you know what they are like. They must know, no matter the cost, not that it is *them* this is costing."

I nodded emphatically and smiled to my mentor, doing all I could to heed his words, though I admit I was oscillating rather between abject horror at the prospect of what I might find, and overenthusiastic excitement at the very same thought.

"I'll be safe," I assured him.

"Ellie... are you ready for this?" he asked me sternly. Thinking on it all now, I believe he asked me that not because he wanted to know the answer or because he felt I needed reassuring. He asked me that because he wanted reassurance. He wanted me to answer that question in such a way that he would feel safer, that he would feel I was to be safe.

But no answer could satisfy that hope.

13

If I said no, of course that would mean I was not ready and that would give him no relief.

Yet I knew well that if I said yes... it would bring no peace either. How can one separate overconfidence and clarity in the mind of another? How can one separate such things within oneself?

So, I did not answer him. I knew no answer would suffice, so I starved him of one. Instead, I leaned forwards and I met his gaze. I stared deep into my mentor's kind, loving, dark eyes and without saying a single word, I told him I would be alright.

Without needing to resort to something so clunky and ineloquent as the spoken word, I met Father Martin's gaze and I told him it would be alright.

He met my gaze too and I think we shared an exchange in that moment, a brief moment of union between our minds, something which I do not feel I can put into words, something which no language can express or explain, but I felt that in that moment we understood one another's souls, and he saw within me a potential which in truth I didn't even see myself.

Then the moment passed. We both leaned back a little, and he nodded calmly, a peaceful smile hinted at by the very corners of his lips.

"Very well," he concluded. "You are ready."

I smiled to him fondly and he smiled back, though still there was pain behind his eyes.

"Go, you had best pack and get ready," he encouraged me.

***

The journey to Scotland was itself a dull affair and so I shall not bother recounting many details of it, suffice to say that I took a train from Rome to Bologna, then to Munich, then another to Cologne, then Brussels, then Calais where I took a ferry to Dover, then another train to London, then Edinburgh, then Perth and finally to Inverness.

I left Rome at 5pm and after over a day and a half of trains and ferries, I arrived in Inverness at around 7am on 10th January 1951. By that point I had read every word in the stack of files given to me by Father Martin, and certainly it had darkened my mood.

First of all, I read a little about the history of the convent. It had been built almost four hundred years earlier, in 1565, by Catholic monks who had fled north to Inverness a decade earlier to escape Protestant England under the reign of Elizabeth I. The convent had gone through alternating stages of use and abandonment over the convening decades as Catholicism and Protestantism fought for command of Britain. The convent was finally settled in again by a mission of Catholic nuns from Glasgow in 1879. The same sisterhood of nuns maintained the convent until the fire in 1947, four years ago.

Overall, the convent had spent in total almost a century as an abandoned old monastery, with its longest continuous period of inoccupation being some thirty years in the mid-1600s. What exactly happened to the building during that time was never made clear, and though the documents I read certainly seemed to try desperately to ignore the glaring issue, I noticed a small footnote which mentioned that when the Glaswegian nuns reclaimed the site in 1879, they had been forced to remove several desecrating marks of cultic relevance and re-sanctify the grounds of the church. It seemed clear that someone, or something, had spent time in that building during its abandonment. Something that the Church greatly wanted to forget about and wanted to keep me from discovering.

I remembered thinking about it at the time, and wondering if it were possible that those cultic symbols and the necessity for the re-sanctification of the grounds might be linked to whatever had happened in 1947. The more documents I read and the longer I spent trying to work out what may have come to occur in that strange place, certainly the more the events seemed that they may be linked.

Next, I read the various accounts from the various locals who had kindly gone up to the convent with pails of water to help combat the flames, to no avail.

The fire had burned on through the night, having begun shortly after dusk, and continued into the morning. By noon the following day the flames had all sputtered out and given up and the locals were able to trawl through the ruins in search of survivors, though in truth they expected only to find bodies.

Their searches, sadly, uncovered no surprises. They found only burnt carcasses. Twenty-five nuns had perished in the fires, with only two of them escaping. Now, without the context of the missing priests or the convent's history, this appeared to be a tragedy but nothing overtly supernatural, and certainly after the fire first happened, the Church would not have been thinking of old histories of the building and they had not yet sent any priests. The thing which led my superiors to start investigating the more supernatural side of things was the testimonies given by the two nuns that escaped.

Sister Bathsheba and Sister Clementina were the only two survivors of the fire, and even then they were afflicted with terrible burns and smoke-filled lungs which would certainly leave them choking for breath for years to come. They had both been moved away to other convents in other places after the incident, so I had no chance of speaking to them myself but... after reading their testimonies, I suspected they would not want to speak with me in any event.

Even now, after seventy years, I have copies of those documents, so I needn't try and remember word for word what I read all those years ago. Below I've copied down the transcripts of the police interview with Sister Bathsheba.

***

Transcript of Police interview with

Sister Bathsheba Royle of St. Agnes Convent, Inverness

by

Chief Inspector Ryan Godrick, Inverness Police Force

17th May 1947

Regarding the fire at St. Agnes Convent, Inverness and the deaths of 25 nuns.

C.I. RYAN GODRICK:

Good evening, Sister, my name is Chief Inspector Ryan Godrick from the Inverness Police Force, how are you feeling this evening?

SISTER BATHSHEBA ROYLE:

I'm not sure, inspector. Rather tired I think.

GODRICK:

Quite understandable, Sister. I'm terribly sorry for your loss, and I imagine this is the last thing you'd like to talk about, but I hope you understand I've got to ask you about what happened. Now, to be entirely clear with you, this is not being treated as a criminal case. We are not, at this time, assuming that anybody had intent to burn down the convent, we just need to know what happened. Can you do that for me?

BATHSHEBA:

You assume wrong.

GODRICK:

Pardon me?

BATHSHEBA:

I said… you assume wrong.

GODRICK:

I'm afraid I don't understand, what do I assume wrong?

BATHSHEBA:

You said you were not assuming anybody wanted to burn the place down. That's just another way of

17

saying you assume it was an accident. You assume wrong.

GODRICK:

You think somebody wanted to burn down a convent full of nuns?

BATHSHEBA:

I know it.

GODRICK:

Who? If you have any information about the person responsible for this, you must tell us.

BATHSHEBA: (beginning to laugh bitterly)

There is nothing you little men in your blue uniforms can do. Nothing!

GODRICK:

Excuse me?

BATHSHEBA:

It was no man that burnt the place down. No man at all! No man looks like that...

GODRICK:

Sister, I fear you may still be in shock. I'd like to end this session now and speak with you at a later date, perhaps when you're feeling a little better.

BATHSHEBA:

Ha! You think because I know more than you that I am mistaken. Only fools think like that. Fools and men. I tell you, I am in no shock and I am not deceived or mistaken or mad. Last night... I saw it... I saw that against which we fight, I saw the very reason for why we sisters gather to pray, to defend against. It came! Into the convent, it came…

GODRICK:

Sister, I'm afraid you've lost me.

BATHSHEBA:

Chief Inspector, last night I witnessed something which I know I will bear witness to again and again every night in my sleep for as long as I shall live. Last night, something came… no… something was summoned into the convent from the very depths of Hell…

GODRICK:

To be clear, you believe this… thing that was… summoned… that is what caused the fire?

BATHSHEBA:

Yes.

GODRICK:

Who would do that? Why?

BATHSHEBA:

Why? To spit in the face of our most Holy God! As for who… the girl is dead now, perished in the fires that came from her own foolishness. I see no point in exposing her now. There is nothing you people can do to punish her, her fate is in God's hands now.

GODRICK:

And you think one of your fellow sisters summoned this… thing…?

BATHSHEBA:

Yes.

GODRICK:

    To spit in the face of God?

BATHSHEBA:

    Yes.

GODRICK:

    And you know who did it, but you won't say out of
    respect for the dead?

BATHSHEBA:

    Yes.

GODRICK:

    I see… very well, Sister, thank you for your time.
    I'm going to end our session here, do you have any
    further comments?

BATHSHEBA:

    Yes. Don't tell the Church about this. They mustn't
    know. They'll only send silly priests to bless the
    place and reclaim it. Boys. Don't tell them. Better
    for their own safety.

GODRICK:

    I'm afraid the convent is owned by the Catholic
    Church, it is their property, so we have a duty to
    inform them of the incident. If that's all, we can
    end this meeting.

BATHSHEBA:

    They mustn't know.

GODRICK:

    I have to tell them. I think that's all for this
    evening. Thank you, Sister. We will be in contact
    if we need anything further. In the meantime, we

will pay for you to stay in The Bloody Stallion Inn
in Ashton.

***

I suppose it was always entirely possible that Sister Bathsheba Royle was delusional or in shock after the incident, but the combination of the seven missing priests – which she seemed to have predicted – and the fact I had been sent here made it clear to me that Bathsheba knew well of what she spoke. Clearly, it seemed, something really might have been summoned to the convent all those years ago.

The most damning evidence, however, I felt, was Sister Clementina's testimony. Sister Bathsheba may have been a little shaken by the ordeal, but Clementina had been positively driven mad. The transcript from her interview with Godrick was largely just a series of adjectives and body parts. "Big", "hairy", "horns", "hooves", "teeth", "fire".

Whatever had gone to the convent that night, both sisters had seen it and one of them had been driven mad.

I could see now why the Church had been so anxious to send so many priests up there.

Finally, I read the police report from that night. Ryan Godrick himself had written it up, and it seemed he was entirely dismissive of both of the survivor's accounts of what happened, though he did attach both transcripts. The man, it seemed, was an atheist with no interest in warning the Church and its priests of monsters.

A pity. Perhaps if he had listened to the nuns, seven priests would still have lived.

I finished reading all these things and pieced together in my mind a narrative for the convent through its long and strange history. I was entirely convinced that both surviving nuns really had witnessed what they described, and indeed that somebody had summoned something to the convent four years ago.

21

In that case... it was my job to get rid of it. My first ever case, and I had to get rid of some spirit or creature which had burnt down a convent and murdered twenty-five nuns, which had caused the disappearances of seven priests, and I had to do it alone.

In that case, what I needed were facts and details. I needed to know what had been summoned, who had summoned it and to what end. I needed to find out exactly what had happened to those seven priests, and, most crucially, I needed to make sure it was still in the ruins of the convent.

I arrived in Inverness early in the morning, around 7am, and was met at the train station by a young gentleman with a donkey and an applecart who had been paid in advance to bring me to Ashton, the little town near which stood the ruins of the convent. The donkey ride was a further hour and by the time we arrived it was 8am.

I had arrived. Now it was time to begin my inquiry.

Chapter 2: The Initial Investigation in Inverness

Ashton was a remarkably small village with maybe two hundred houses, a small post office – which, when I arrived, was shut – a public library which seemed to have been abandoned and foreclosed sometime around its own opening, a village hall, a small police station with an attached jail – which my documents had informed me was about as useful as the public library – and the largest building in the village; the inn named The Bloody Stallion.

The village was laid out vaguely in the shape of a cross with a small green in the heart of the village square and the inn, the village hall and the police station as near to the centre as each could get. I decided that the best place to go first would probably be the police station, to make myself known to the local authorities. My conscious reasoning at the time was that if some strange nun was going to go poking about the village asking questions, it was worth letting the authorities know beforehand, just so that I might gauge whether or not they'd be any use should the locals get upset about my questions.

Looking back on it all now, however, I think I subconsciously reasoned that, when and if I went missing, it was worth at the very least making sure the Church knew that I'd actually made it to Ashton.

The kind boy with the donkey dropped me off just by the village green at the centre of the crossroads in the heart of the village, before turning away and clopping back up the road the way he and his donkey had come. I had a black leather briefcase, emblazoned with the cross on both sides, filled with a few clean habits, the stacks of paperwork and a few books and Bibles, and that was all but for the clothes on my back. I was, of course, a nun. We were not expected to own much. I picked up my briefcase and marched across the village square with authoritative determination. I know I got numerous strange looks from the locals of course; a fairly short little nun barely more than five feet tall, marching across the square with a purpose, but I didn't much care how they saw me. I was here to do a job and that was all.

23

I stepped up into the small, shabby, ramshackle sort of old redbrick building which the dreary, dirty sign outside informed me was supposed to be a police station, and smiled kindly to the officer on duty, a little, plump sort of man with a grey beard down to his belly and a scalp that did a wonderful little impression of the moon. He had hard, beady sort of eyes and stared intently through small, narrow, wire-frame glasses that perched on the end of his nose, hardly wide enough for his broad, thick head. The object of his intense stare was a broadsheet newspaper which he held out from himself, completely spread out as if trying to hide behind it from anybody – such as myself – who might come into the station. He was leaning back in his chair far enough that I thought it a miracle he hadn't gone end over apex backwards and cracked his head on the wall behind him, and all these things together made me rather think he was an altogether useless policeman.

"Ahem," I coughed quietly.

"Aye?" he asked me rudely, not for a moment glancing up from his broadsheet. He had a thick, deep Scottish brogue that almost made the ground beneath me rumble.

"I'd like to speak with you chief officer, my name is-," I began before rudely being cut off by the man.

"I *am* the chief officer. And I'm busy, can I take a name to schedule an appointment with later?" he asked me boredly, flicking over to the next page of his newspaper.

"I am Sister Eleanor Jesse, investigator of the supernatural. I've been sent by the Vatican to investigate the incident at the convent four years ago and the seven missing priests," I told the officer in as an official of a voice as I could muster. "And you don't seem busy in the slightest."

"Investigator of the what?" the officer asked dryly, clearly taking me less and less seriously by the second. "Sounds like cooks and hooey to me."

"Investigator of the supernatural. The closest a woman can get to being an Exorcist," I told him icily. "My word, man, seven priests have gone missing and you're sitting a mile from the burnt-down ruins of a convent in which twenty-five nuns died and you're going to sit there and read a paper without even looking at me. What sort of chief are you?"

That got his attention.

"The convent burning down was a tragedy. It really was. But Chief Inspector Godrick from them city folk in Inverness said it was an accident and nothing more. If he said it was an accident, it was an accident. As for them priests... the convent's up in the hills and that's the last place any of them went in this town. You sound English to me, even if you are from the Vatican. You southerners always underestimate the bears up here. I imagine they were all eaten. If they were lucky the bears went for the throat and took them out nice and quick. Now, unless you want to be bear food, I recommend you drop this whole thing and get out of my village," the chief told me coldly, having finally stood up and come to lean over the desk to sneer down in my face. "Got it, lassie?"

I confess I was rather frightened of him, but I didn't dare let that show, not for a second.

"What's your name?" I asked him calmly.

"Does it matter?" he asked with the same rude, indignant aggression as before.

"You know my name, I'd like to know who I'm speaking to," I reasoned to him calmly.

"Chief Constable Adrian McIntosh," he responded gruffly.

"Well, Chief Constable Adrian McIntosh, I'll be careful to watch out for bears when I go up to the convent this afternoon. I don't care how much you may want me to turn and flee, I was sent here by the Vatican, sent here by God to find out what happened up there and, if at all possible, save the seven priests. If it is too late to save their lives then at the very least I might give them their last rites and set them to rest and save their souls. I am here

25

under the orders of God and no institution of man will stop me. If you want me to leave this place promptly, then you'll help me to speed my investigation along the way!" I told him, remaining calm throughout, but taking on a stern and authoritative tone as I went.

I had spent the last decade being talked down to by men; priests and bishops and all sorts looked down at me as a lowly little nun. I'd never spoken back to them, of course, but bitten my tongue and found angry, eloquent retorts to hiss at the walls of my chambers or into my reflection in the mirror. Now, at last, I could talk back to a man in a way I had never been able to before.

McIntosh, it seemed, was unsure of how to respond to an angry nun standing up for herself. I suppose he was considering locking me up, but we both knew it wouldn't look very good for him if Chief Inspector Godrick – who seemed to be McIntosh's boss – were to come down only to find an innocent nun locked up in the cells.

At last, McIntosh sat back down and disappeared back into his newspaper.

"On second thoughts," he grumbled. "I hope the bears take their time, do it slow. Maybe that'll teach you some manners."

"I am not the one who needs to learn my manners," I retorted, turning to leave before he could say another word.

Just as I passed through the door, I left him with one final remark, "oh, and by the looks of your police station, the bears have already been!"

A moment later, I was out of the station and stood in the middle of the village green, taking deep breaths and trying hard to steel myself after the confrontation had left me feeling rather flustered.

McIntosh was indeed about as useful of a policeman as a blunt pencil. On second thoughts, a pencil could be sharpened so perhaps he was even more useless.

I stood there, alone in the square for a few moments, thinking what I might best do next. I could have headed up to the convent directly, I thought, but I was wary of going up there without getting a better idea of what I might find, and if McIntosh was telling me the truth about bears in the hills, then I didn't suppose I'd want to be going up there on my own.

I needed to find a friend then, someone who knew the lands well, knew the local stories well and knew the hills well. Someone local then, and ideally someone well-versed in the village gossip.

So, I made my way over towards the local tavern, The Bloody Stallion Inn. My travel documents said that a telegram had been sent ahead to book lodging for me in that inn and, I recalled from the other documents in my briefcase, that was the place Sister Bathsheba had lodged briefly after the fire.

The way McIntosh had spoken... there was something about that convent that the locals didn't like. It wasn't just that he was lazy... he had insisted I leave the village... the locals knew something about that convent, certainly they knew more than the Chief Constable had been prepared to share with me.

I suspected I'd find someone in the inn who might have the same knowledge, but perhaps someone a little more friendly.

The building was, as I said, the largest in the village by far; an enormous old house with a redbrick ground floor and several black and white storeys above it like an old Victorian house, topped by a thatched roof. Several smaller sorts of buildings like cottages came off the sides of it, including a stable, and the overall feel of the inn perfectly encapsulated the entire sense which filled Ashton; which was that it was like stepping back in time.

Even in 1951, we had cars and telephones and all sorts of luxuries of that sort, but in Ashton... I was tremendously grateful to learn that they *did* have indoor plumbing and relatively modern toilets, but the place felt rather like a step back in time a further fifty years, as though this were 1901, not 1951. Looking back on it all now, another seventy years later in 2021, that village seems so ancient. I haven't been there in a long time, perhaps I should visit it some time. I wonder if the locals will know me from their legends, or if the village has entirely forgotten about what happened there seventy years ago.

At any rate... I entered the tavern, striding in confidently through its big, oak double doors.

I thought I was so clever, but there was one obvious thing I hadn't considered; I was a nun.

The moment some cross-laden Catholic nun stepped foot in that tavern, one might've heard a pin drop from a mile off. The general hubbub and chattering that I had heard halfway across the street suddenly disappeared as soon as I walked in the door and I felt at least a dozen angry, judgemental pairs of eyes fall upon me.

A lone nun walks into a bar... I'm sure there's a joke about that...

I was uncomfortable under the staring gaze, but I had a job to do. I was just relieved that it was still before nine in the morning. The inn was mostly empty but for a handful of big, burly Scotsmen drinking away their sorrows. I was a little surprised to find the tavern populated at all this early in the morning on a Wednesday, even considering the fact I was in Scotland I had expected the place to be more or less barren. My plan *had* been to take my things up to my room and to pray and wait until the ground floor filled up a bit, but...

I gulped a little, I confess, and took a breath to steel my nerves before boldly striding into the pub and taking a place at the bar. The barkeep came over and leaned across the bar. He was a fairly young man, cleanshaven with ruffled black hair and weary brown eyes that didn't match his youthful appearance. At a guess I'd have said he was only a few years younger than me, somewhere between twenty and twenty-five I think. He was fairly fashionably dressed with a black waistcoat and black trousers and a pocket-watch chain showing, though all his clothes were a little stained and there was a faint whiff of ale about him, though that might have just been the inn... or the country...

"I don't suppose you'll be wanting anything strong, sister," the barkeep chuckled to himself. His accent was a little milder and his voice far softer than

McIntosh's, and I got the sense that, in his youth, the barkeep was still a tender and gentle soul.

"Not this early in the morning. Perhaps later," I replied kindly. "Some water will do."

"I thought you lot didn't drink alcohol at all," he replied as he started pouring me a pint of water.

"The Lord asked us for chastity, poverty and honesty. Alcohol was never mentioned," I responded, joking a little though what I said was still true. "Somebody has to drink the leftover communion wine, what else are priests for?"

He laughed at that, a proper, loud laugh. "That's very true, I hadn't thought of that before. I don't suppose I need to ask you what brings you here. You're the first nun they've sent, but it's still a giveaway."

I nodded as I sipped my water. It was a little bitter-tasting but no worse than I had grown up with in Liverpool. "St. Agnes Convent."

The young man's face turned sour like a switch. "We don't much talk about that place round here."

I looked around. I half expected for the other locals to be glaring me to death but most of them were sharing quiet conversations in hushed tones, or were simply passed out in their booths.

"My apologies. McIntosh gave me a certain impression of the town's view on the convent, but I didn't realise it was so taboo," I bowed my head in solemn apology to the young man.

He shrugged. "Oh, don't let that old idiot frighten you off. McIntosh is about as bright as a ball of lead and the only time he's done any actual policing round here was when he finally worked out his wife had been cheating on him for thirty years. The rest of the village had known a good decade before that so... he's not exactly bright. Mostly he just sits on his fat ar- uh... sits on

29

his backside… and pretends like he's important. Pardon my slip-up there sister…"

I smiled to the boy. He was kind, and certainly he was far more polite than McIntosh had been.

"Quite alright," I laughed. "He was sat on his arse when I went to see him earlier."

The young man laughed again, a proper Scottish belt of laughter.

"You're an odd nun," he mused.

I shrugged. "It's been said."

I had already decided by this point that I'd like to have this young chap accompany me up to the ruins; he was friendly enough and seemed like a smart boy well-versed in local knowledge who might be handy to question and to help scare off the bears.

"What's your name?" he asked me politely, his hand outstretched.

"Sister Eleanor," I told him with equal politeness, shaking his hand. "And yours?"

"Archie Wood."

After shaking hands, Archie rummaged about beneath the bar for a moment for a stool, on which he sat just across from me.

"I take it you're here like those priests, here to go poking about… up there…?" he asked me quietly, clearly finding a great deal of discomfort in the very thought of naming the location of my expedition.

"I am. Seven priests have come here and gone missing, and it's getting into more and more of a problem for the Vatican. They want me to go up there and find out where the priests have gone and, if I can, to save them," I explained to him with equal discretion.

"There's something up there," he told me plainly. "I mean... you probably already know that, but... there's something up there. Not just in the hills, though there's plenty of stories about what's in the hills. I mean in the... in that place... there's something that wasn't there before. Four years ago, it came..."

"What came?" I asked.

Archie shook his head.

"No. Not here. I'll be run out of town if my boss catches me talking about that place... to a nun of all people... no offence..." Archie whispered, shaking his head.

"Can you tell me later? Somewhere else?" I asked, now quite certain that Archie was the man I wanted to take up to the ruins with me.

Archie paused a moment to think. "I finish at ten tonight, when the place starts getting lively. If you're happy to wait that long, I can find you and we can talk in private then."

"Would you be willing to take me up to the ruins?" I asked him.

Archie almost fell off his stool in shock. "No. No way. Nobody goes up there. Nobody. Never. You're welcome to try but... well... like I said, we have plenty of stories that can tell you what lives up in those hills. I'll come talk to you later but I won't take you up there, no. And you're not likely to find anybody else willing to take you neither."

I bit my lip in frustration, but decided now was not the time for rash thinking or desperately trying to convince the boy to help. God wanted me in those ruins, so I had faith God would find a way to get me there safely, that is; with company.

"Very well. I'd still like to talk later if you're willing," I asked. Archie nodded.

"In that case, could you show me to my room? The Vatican telegrammed ahead," I asked. Archie nodded again. He got up, replaced his stool under the bar, and started searching about in a stack of papers until he found the telegram, which he then used to navigate through a cupboard of keys, clearly looking for the one to my room. Eventually, he found the right one and came around the bar to escort me up the stairs.

"May I carry your luggage?" he asked. I shook my head.

"I'm a nun. We travel light," I smiled.

"Very good," Archie nodded and began to lead me around the corner and up the stairs. We climbed two or three flights before finally reaching a long, narrow corridor which I could only presume was in the attic, and came to a door at the very end of the hallway. Archie unlocked the door for me and with a flourish welcomed me to my room.

It was a small, drab, old, rundown sort of room, with windows that rattled in the breeze and air as cold as the grave. The walls and floor were creaky old planks of wood that groaned seemingly for no reason and the furniture looked all about a hundred years old; a rickety old single bed with a rickety desk and a rickety chest of draws. The room was cramped and damp and overall quite miserable.

Yet somehow, I felt wonderfully... at home... in that place and I cannot think to say why. It seemed to me quite simply that I was so excited to finally be on my very own first case. The room was not where I felt at home. The job was.

I thanked Archie and closed the door as he traipsed off down the corridor and down the stairs, and finally I took a deep breath and sighed.

I was here.

I was on my first case.

I opened up my briefcase and began unpacking my things, putting my spare habits in the chest of draws and lining up the Bibles and books along the desk. I deposited the stack of documents alongside the books such that it and the wall could act as bookends.

Then I sat on the edge of my bed, closed my eyes, and began to pray.

"Good morning, Lord," I began warmly. "I made it! You knew that of course... I just hope you've got a plan to get me up to those ruins safely. I really would rather not be eaten by bears so I'd appreciate it if, in your holy divinity and all-knowing ways, you wouldn't mind convincing that Archie boy to take me up there. He certainly seems to know the place and the people well, and he's a good boy to chat with, if only he could be convinced to take me up there, it would be wonderfully appreciated. If not him, I'm sure you'll give me somebody else as a guide, I just pray that I'll know who it is so I can befriend them. I suppose then I pray that you'll guide me towards what actions I can take to best enact your plan, and that I will be receptive to your voice when you speak to me."

I paused, trying to think.

"I'd also like to pray for Father Martin. His health is failing already and all this stress as he worries about me... it cannot be good for him. It would be appreciated if you were to give him a little encouragement and reassurance. Speaking of which, I pray for your protection in all this. Seven priests have, of course, gone missing already, seven far, far more experienced priests than I. In all honesty, I don't stand a chance, do I? But, as David stood before Goliath with nothing but a sling and a pebble, he was armed with nothing but faith, and now so am I. I pray you will grant me the same fortunes as you granted David all those years ago," I prayed.

Even then, I didn't see prayer as something one should make a formal affair. Many other nuns and monks and priests who I know like to speak to God as one speaks to one's boss, but while Jesus may well be our boss, he is also our friend. He knows all my innermost thoughts, so to hide my true feelings with false politeness is an absurdity. And so, I keep my prayers open and honest and sincere. I spoke to God as a friend to confide in, not a mighty authority to lie to and humbly beg.

"I'm anxious, Lord," I continued after a moment of quiet reflection. "I know I can do this, I have every faith in myself to get this job done, to find out what happened and bring it to an end, but… I do not know if I am mistaking pride for determination. I pray for your guidance, God. I think I know what to do… help me, God."

I put my head in my hands and took a breath for a moment. I stood and peered out the window. I looked about at the town, at the people, and took it all in for a moment.

I closed my eyes and tried to empty myself of my own identity and let the identity of the village and the people of Ashton fill me, I tried to be one with them, to understand their fears and hopes and dreams and nightmares.

I fell down as I suddenly felt something grabbing at my throat. There was nothing there and yet I had, for just a second, felt something throttling me, like a hand had reached through the window to attack me… but there was, of course, nothing…

"God, these people are afraid," I said as I felt a great, overwhelming horror and depression seize my heart, but the feelings were not mine. I had absorbed the heart of the village and that was its contents; fear and sadness. Not just sadness, but… despair. Hopelessness. "God, I need your guidance. I need to help these people. Help me help them. Please."

I think in that moment I witnessed a glimpse of what my job really was. I was here to find things beyond mortal understanding and to combat them, yes, but not with the motive of simply thwarting darkness. I was here to save these people. The Church had lost seven priests to those ruins… but what had the people of Ashton lost? The despair that hung over the town… it was palpable. The very air suddenly seemed rich with dread. What had that thing in the ruins done to this town?

I was here to help them.

That was the feeling that made this place seem like my home, not the building or the thought of fighting evil… just the thought of helping people. I could make a real difference in that town, I knew I could. I intended to enact upon that potential.

"God, guide me to help these people," I prayed. "Amen."

* * *

After concluding my prayers, I pottered about for a little while, perhaps twenty or thirty minutes, before finally deciding I was quite exhausted after more than a day of constant travel, and decided that it was time I had a little nap. By now it was almost noon, and I recalled that Archie had said he would be available again after ten that evening, so I elected to get as many hours of sleep as I could, having barely slept at all on the trains thanks to fears of being robbed or harmed, and I suspected I would not have much time to sleep that night if I was to travel to the ruins of the convent with Archie as I had hoped I might.

And so, for the day, I was like an owl; a nocturnal creature of the darkness who slept in the light of the sun and would awake in the moonlight.

I slept for a good eight or nine hours I think, after spending another twenty or so minutes calming my thoughts and drifting away to sleep. It was around nine in the evening, or shortly after, when I awoke.

I quickly changed into a fresh habit, having realised I had just slept in the one I'd been wearing for travelling over the last day or so, and got myself ready to speak with Archie about the convent. I decided that I would want a notebook and a pen in order to jot down the key facts which he might share, as well as a Bible and a few spare rosaries. By ten, I was finally prepared and a few moments later, I heard heavy, hard boots come traipsing up the stairs and along the corridor.

"God, please give me the words to convince him to accompany me," I prayed silently and quickly as I heard a knock upon the door.

My prayer, as it turned out, had already been answered.

I opened the door to see Archie, with a thick, heavy coat, thick boots, warm trousers and a furry hat on, stood in the doorway with a shotgun in hand.

"I know there's no stopping you going to those ruins, and I know nobody else in this town will take you, and I'd rather you weren't eaten by bears in the dark, so... I'll take you up there," he grumbled, clearly a little baffled by his own decision, but having made up his mind about it anyway.

I smiled.

God, it seemed, wanted me in those ruins as much as I wanted to be there.

"Thank you, Archie, you're terribly kind," I smiled to him gratefully.

"Or terribly stupid. One of the two," he shrugged. "You'll want something a little warmer than a habit, though. Do you have a coat or anything?"

I shook my head.

I had forgotten that Scotland was cold.

Archie rolled his eyes glumly. "I'll find something in the pub for you. When we get downstairs, wait outside. Use the back door at the bottom of the stairs, I don't want any of the locals working out where I'm taking you. There'll be a riot and they'll have my guts for garters if they know."

I nodded emphatically, overjoyed that my prayers had been answered, and followed Archie along the corridor and down the stairs to the pub, before discretely depositing myself out in the cold via the little back door at the bottom of the stairs.

The night was dark, with air like ice and a chilling wind whistling through the little village on the south shores of Loch Ashie.

The sky above was black as charcoal, filled with thick, rolling blankets of thunderclouds and every now and again I heard a distant grumble of thunder, though oddly enough I never saw a single flash of lightning. I shivered in the freezing cold, though I supposed I had only myself to blame for not packing a coat on a trip to Scotland. I was ever so grateful when, a moment later, Archie emerged with a big, thick woman's winter coat with a fur trim, within which I was able to seclude myself. One of the benefits of being barely more than five feet tall was that I was able to quite effortlessly swaddle myself in the otherwise average-sized coat as though it were an enormous robe.

Archie smirked, and I suppose I can't blame him. I imagine I looked quite ridiculous; a tiny little nun all wrapped up in a big, thick coat, but at least now I was warm.

"Ready?" he asked, chuckling still.

"Yes," I nodded vigorously, anxious to get going.

"The ruins are about a mile northwest, but they're up in the hills and the terrain is… rough… so it'll take us about an hour to get there, is that alright?" he asked me. I sensed that he was trying to make me doubt the plan, but I was set on going up to those ruins there and then, and there was no changing my mind.

"Yes, that's fine," I nodded again.

"Alright then," Archie shrugged, I think seeming a little disappointed. He then reached up, to a little lantern that hung down from a hook above the back door, and unhooked it, giving us a source of light. "Let's go."

Archie led me away through the backstreets of Ashton, sneaking around through the dark to avoid the locals. He took me through all manner of alleyways and twisting, winding, steep uphill lanes between warm old stone cottages, fancy modern redbrick buildings, and old, timber houses and schools. Finally, we seemed to leave the old village behind entirely and disappeared into the woods. The wind was just as harsh in the trees as it had been in the town, but now the air somehow had grown colder, and I started to think I'd be getting icicles hanging from my nose!

We stumbled in half blindness through the trees for quite a while, tripping on roots and fallen branches of the undergrowth again and again as the little lantern failed to produce much in the way of actual light, all the while the ground beneath our feet gradually getting steeper and steeper. Eventually, we broke through the treeline and came out into a little outcrop at a sort of natural halfway-mark for the hill. Below, the dark trees sloped down to the flickering dim lights of the village of Ashton at the bottom of the hill, with nothing but fields and forest and hills in all directions except north, where there lay the inky black waters of Loch Ashie, which seemed as black as the charcoal storm clouds overhead.

Again, I heard a great boom of thunder, but there was no lightning to cause it, an event I found to be very odd indeed.

Even in the darkness, however, I must admit the scene was beautiful. There was something ominous about the storm overhead and the unforgiving black waters of Loch Ashie that made the place somehow seem... peaceful, but temporary, like the blissful calm before a terribly violent storm.

"This way," Archie directed me, and we set off along a pathway through the trees which seemed to wrap around the hill.

"So," I began.

"Yes?"

"I take it you've lived in Ashton a while, since before the convent burned down at least?" I asked, beginning what I would have called an interview, though I imagine Archie might have preferred 'interrogation'.

"Yeah. Was born here, live here, probably die here. That's what everyone does. We're born here, we stay here, eventually we die here. Small towns like this, there's no escape, I'm telling you," he responded a little glumly. I nodded my head slowly, thinking of another question.

"You were in town on that night, four years ago?" I asked.

Archie nodded.

"I was one of the men that brought pails of water up to the convent. The sky was orange, you could see it from the town. We all ran up there with buckets and pails of water, we were desperate to help. But the place was too far away and by the time we could tell something was wrong... well, like I said, we only knew because the sky was orange. The flames were already out of control. We went up anyway, of course, but there wasn't much to be done. Sister Bathsheba and Sister Clementina were already out of there, choking and coughing for air out on the edge of the forest. Everyone else...," Archie tried to explain to me, but his voice began to fade away to nothing. Clearly those were memories he was uncomfortable recalling. I only wished I could have done my job without pressing him further.

"You did all you could. It wasn't your fault, none of you," I reassured him. Archie shrugged and nodded slowly.

"The police said it was some sort of chemical accident," Archie said, clearly trying to shift the subject. I was content to let him.

"Yes. Sister Myrtle apparently had a laboratory in which she performed scientific experiments. Chief Inspector Godrick from the city said that's where the fire started. I'd certainly like to go in and have a look," I recalled from memory. Archie nodded, as if he'd heard some of that before.

"What did the priests do when they came here?" I asked. "I know more or less what happened four years ago, but what happened to the missing priests? The Church knows nothing."

Archie shrugged. "They more or less all did the same thing I think. They came to town, made friendly with the locals, stayed a night in The Bloody Stallion, tried and failed to get on McIntosh's good side – failed because he hasn't got one, he just has a bad side and a worse side – and eventually, one by one, they went up to the ruins. Alone."

"I see," I responded, taking a moment to process that. I was, at least, bucking the trend already. I wasn't going up alone. I wondered if that would be enough to set in motion an entirely different set of events and, I prayed, might see this case ending not with my death but with a triumph. "And they never came back down?"

"Oh, no, they did. They all came back down. From their first visit, at least. They always came back down from the first visit. Then they'd spend another night sleeping on it and head up the next day again… and that's when it happened. Every time. That's when it happened," Archie answered with an ominous sense of dread, as though he wanted to tell me about something awful, but at the same time he wanted to forget it all entirely.

"What happened?" I asked.

Archie shrugged. "Bad stuff. There's a reason we don't talk about that place."

"I need you to be specific," I urged him. "It could be important."

Archie stopped in his tracks and sighed. "Jodie Jones is the youngest child in the village. She turned three last May. She was born a few days after the fire. After that… there hasn't been a single other child born in Ashton. Not for nearly four years now."

I frowned, realising that whatever I was about to be told… it was going to be dark news.

"Every time a priest goes up there for his second visit… a few hours after he's last seen… every woman in the whole village. Every pregnant woman… all of them… no matter how many of them happen to be pregnant at the time… they all miscarry, all at once, every single one of them. There's maybe three hundred… four hundred people in this village. There's been about forty… fifty pregnancies in the last four years, since the fire. But no new babies. No children. Every time a priest went up for his second visit, every woman miscarried, all at once. Seven times it's happened. Fifty miscarriages. A lot of them are the same women, desperate to have a baby before the next priest comes along. The women miscarry and the priests don't come back. That's why we hate that place. We know something's up there, we know it's killing our children. That's why McIntosh was so desperate to get rid of you. But he's afraid, we all are. We know something's up there, but who's going to actually admit it? We've all just agreed without agreeing… agreed to keep silent. Agreed not to talk about it, to just pretend nothing's wrong…," Archie explained to me, at times breaking up, his voice falling into wavering cracks and whimpers as he clearly struggled desperately to convey to me the immense… sadness… which he felt.

I understood then why the heart of Ashton had been a ball of fear and pain and despair.

They were losing their children.

"I'm so sorry, Archie," I said, though I found there was nothing I could do or say to convey my overwhelming sense of apology.

He sniffled a little and wiped a tear from his eye.

"You're not like the priests. That's why I'm helping you. I'd like to be a father eventually, and there's just something... if there's anybody that can fight this, something tells me it's you," Archie mumbled, wiping his nose in his sleeve.

I smiled, rather touched by his kind words. "Thank you."

He nodded. "Yeah well... the ruins are this way."

He pointed up ahead and carried on. I followed after, deciding to take a moment to breathe before continuing with my questions.

The night certainly seemed darker now, and the air was immeasurably colder and windier, and yet... the trees were still. In fact, aside from our own footsteps and the sound of the wind rushing past us and ruffling our clothes, there was nothing, only silence. Still trees and an empty undergrowth.

Again, the world seemed to tremble as a terrible peal of thunder roared from somewhere overhead, yet the world remained as black as before, devoid of lightning or a single flare of illumination. Nothing but darkness.

How odd, I thought.

Thunder without lightning, and wind that does not touch the trees. I had left my books and pen in my room after finding out I'd be going on a walk with Archie there and then, but I mentally noted down these strange signs and decided to read about them when we returned to the inn.

"When was the last time you came up here?" I asked.

"The night of the fire," Archie replied, his voice still a little hollow after our previous little chat.

"This must all seem very different to you then," I prompted, my tone as neutral and kind as I could manage.

"Not really. The path hasn't changed, and I grew up taking supplies and messages to and from the convent. I could probably walk this route without the lantern, though I wouldn't want to try it," Archie shrugged casually. I just nodded, realising that the conversation had started to bubble down into small talk. Archie was still terribly uncomfortable talking about the convent. It had taken a lot more out of him than I'd realised to share what he already had, and so I decided to leave the questions for now.

We walked on in silence for a little while, until Archie eventually surprised me with a question of his own.

"Have you seen many things like this before?" he asked me earnestly.

I nodded. "I have. Well... sort of. This is my first proper case of my own, though I've assisted my mentor, Father Martin, on dozens of cases and in plenty of exorcisms."

"Exorcisms?" Archie asked, baffled.

"Yes. A process to drive out dark spirits," I explained briefly.

"Like what?" he asked me.

I supposed it was my turn to dig up buried, painful memories. "Well... the first case I worked with Father Martin... there was this little girl. I think she was seven years old. This was two years ago now..."

I paused, preparing myself to share the tale.

"What happened to her?" Archie asked, fully engaged already. I think really he just wanted a distraction.

"It's not pleasant," I warned him. "It's really, *really* not pleasant."

Archie shrugged. "It can't be worse than what we've got in Ashton."

He had me there.

"Very well... there was a seven-year-old girl named Alice Jackson. Her parents had first noticed something was wrong after a family holiday in Greece. At first, it was little things, things that parents like to dismiss as just children being children. She would act up, getting angry for no reason and throwing great tantrums and five minutes later be just another sweet little girl. Then things got stranger. Alice would start chasing birds from the back garden, almost like she thought she was a cat... her parents thought it was just a game but... then she broke a bird's neck... with her teeth. They took her to a doctor, but there was nothing wrong with her physically. The doctor said the behaviour was unusual but nothing too severe, and encouraged the parents to be patient...," I began.

I knew what was coming. I didn't want to think about what happened next.

"This carried on for a few weeks, until suddenly Alice started acting... older. It was like she was a fifteen-year-old girl rather than seven. She started fighting her mother about how to dress and about boys and... well her parents contacted the Church right after what happened next...," I continued, already uncomfortable with where I knew the story was going.

"What did she do?" Archie asked.

"You have to understand... Alice was possessed. It had started in Greece, but for months she had been the victim of a powerful and hungry Demonic force. First it was appearing to her as an imaginary friend, telling her how to behave and when; twisting her thoughts and her feelings, manipulating her, tricking her into submission, making her weaker... a powerful, ancient, hungry Demon harassing a poor, innocent, seven-year-old girl until... until it took control of her completely. What happened... it wasn't the girl's fault. Alice Jackson never did anything wrong," I said, very sternly and very, very clearly.

Archie nodded in understanding.

43

I took a breath.

"Alice... the Demon possessing her... used Alice to... to molest six other schoolgirls, friends of Alice's. It used that poor little girl to... to do those horrible things. And then... Alice started treating one of the poor girls it had attacked like it had treated the birds. It broke that poor little child's neck and killed her."

"God...," Archie swore.

"God had nothing to do with that, I can promise you," I assured him. "After that... Alice's parents got the Church involved, and Father Martin was summoned, with me in tow. I assisted in the exorcism," I concluded gravely.

"Did it work?" Archie asked, filled with some morbid curiosity. "You said exorcisms were a way of saving people from evil spirits. Did you save the little girl?"

"I said exorcisms were processes to drive out dark spirits. I never said anything about saving anybody. It's an extraordinarily dangerous process, trying to convince an angry, hungry, wretched Demon to leave a person's body. They tend to lash out. Everybody in that room is in grave danger, especially the victim of the possession. It's like trying to defuse a bomb by shooting the wires with a shotgun," I clarified. "Father Martin and I performed the exorcism. The process was a success and the Demon was driven out, yes..."

"And Alice?" Archie asked.

I just shook my head.

I remembered what had happened. I remembered the blood that had washed over the floor, flooding it up to my ankles. I remembered the lifeless, waxy eyes of that little girl as the Demon forced a twisted, unnatural grin onto the face of her corpse. I remembered watching that tiny, twisted, broken little body fly around the room and dance and sing like a marionette on invisible strings. I didn't need to relive it again by telling Archie.

44

"We drove it out, but it was too late. The Demon was too deep in her mind. Alice was too far gone. The best we could do was force the Demon to give up her soul and let the girl rest in peace in the company of her maker. But her life... there was nothing we could do to save her life. We kept the Demon from latching onto anybody else and sent it back to where it came from, but little Alice Jackson... whatever happened to her after the exorcism... that was in God's hands, not ours," I explained glumly. I didn't want to spend a moment longer thinking about that.

"I'm really sorry. I'm sure you did the best you could," Archie said after a moment of silence.

I just nodded. "That's only one example of course. I've helped in plenty of exorcisms, all of which went a lot better. But this case... this isn't like that. Nobody here is possessed as far as I've seen. The ruins may well need exorcising, perhaps, perhaps not, but that poses a threat only to me and anybody in the ruins at the time. Ashton is safe, down in the valley. Your people are safe from that."

"Tell that to our children," Archie grumbled. I realised I must have insulted him by calling his people safe. After everything that town had been through... they must have felt anything but *safe*.

"I'm sorry, I didn't mean...," I apologised.

"It's fine. I'm sorry. You were just trying to reassure me, I know. Forgive me, Sister," Archie smiled through pained eyes.

I smiled back.

"We're here," Archie announced, stopping.

Up ahead, rising up from the ground like monolithic towers of death, were the ruins of St. Agnes Convent, Inverness.

Chapter 3: The Experiments of Sister Myrtle

The ruins of the convent tasted like a bad memory. The very air up there was like the breath of a ghost.

The ruins themselves still stood tall, and indeed the general shape of the ancient, gothic building still held together. The roof had long-since collapsed, both the tiles and its wooden frame completely destroyed, and every window – I am sure they had been beautiful, ornate, stained-glass – had been shattered.

The building was like a grand and royal castle, not truly vast, but still a looming beast of stone and brick with the remains of great, towering spires which had long since burned away and yet still their ghosts seemed to haunt the towers that remained.

The building was, as many such structures often are, built in the shape of a cross with a cloister coming off to one side. The main body of the convent was an architectural work of gothic art, with enormous flying buttresses and wonderfully ornate masonry carved into the centuries-old stonework, now blackened by the smoke and ash of that night. Even after four years, the rains had failed to wash it clean.

The walls of the convent were the same shade of darkness as the charcoal clouds above and the inky waters of Loch Ashie below. There was something altogether sinister about the building too, as if it were somehow alive.

I felt eyes falling upon me, like a room full of people had suddenly fallen silent to stare at us, but the place was empty; abandoned.

There was nothing left but memories.

Bad memories.

The building had left behind ruins and the nuns had left behind their pain. I only prayed that their souls had been pulled from the fires and delivered unto the hands of the Lord before their suffering grew too great.

The wind had picked up again now, blowing all about us, and yet still the trees were still and the night beyond us was silent. I looked over to Archie, who was very clearly uncomfortable with being back in this place.

"Are you alright, Archie?" I asked. He nodded and sort of struggled to peel his gaze away from the ruins and back to me, as though the place had locked him in a trance.

"Yeah, sorry. I'm fine, just... bad memories," he mumbled uncomfortably.

His gaze returned to the ruins and, just for a moment, I could almost see the light of that fire reflected in his eyes, I could almost see his memory of that tragic night, burning through his mind.

"I'm sorry," I gave my condolences.

He just nodded and sniffed, wiping his nose on his sleeve.

"What do you need to do up here?" he asked.

I paused for a moment and thought. "I'd like to have a look about in general, and I definitely need to see Sister Myrtle's laboratory. I think I'll start by examining the consecration of the grounds, so I'd like to look around as much of the ruins as possible, please."

Archie nodded. "This way then."

He led me around the corner and to the great big archway which had, presumably, held a set of double doors to act as the entrance to the convent, now nothing but black stone and charcoal. Archie headed into the convent straight away, but I took a moment to gather my wits and explore my senses, trying to feel any entities or presences that might have been lurking in the dark.

I still felt all those eyes on me, still felt as if dozens of people were standing right there, right in front of me, just in the shadows, not even trying to hide, and as if they were all watching me, just staring right at me, trying to meet my gaze.

Something was here still, that much I was certain of.

Something was watching.

I took a step forwards and crossed the threshold of the convent, entering into its dark halls.

I suddenly felt something else, not being watched, but... I suddenly felt like a hand had reached out from the darkness and grabbed at my throat once more.

I jumped and shouted, leaping backwards and immediately the sensation stopped. The hand let me go.

My own hands of course flew to my throat by instinct, but there was nothing there.

"You okay, Sister?" Archie asked me, concerned.

I steadied my panicked breath and took a moment to compose myself.

"Yes, I'm fine... whatever is here... whatever it is... it knows I'm here. It's watching us," I explained slowly, still catching my breath.

"What do you mean?" Archie asked, frowning in confusion.

"Earlier, in the village, just for a moment, I felt something reach out to me. It grabbed my throat. It was warning me. And again, just now, as I stepped into the convent, I felt it again. Whatever is hiding up here in the convent, it doesn't like my presence," I explained, now having calmed myself a little.

Archie just nodded slowly, clearly he didn't really understand what was going on, but the poor boy was doing his best. Despite his lack of understanding, he clearly had faith in me, and that alongside his company brought me peace and confidence.

I stepped forth again, and while I felt nothing grab at my throat this time, I suddenly felt the wind drop and the air temperature plummet, as though I had just stepped through a gateway into the arctic. I held out my hand, just ahead of me, and I felt the air. It was cold and solid. There was something there, hiding in the very air, too thin to touch, but not too thin to sense. It was as though something had evaporated itself to hide within the very ambience of the ruins.

"Something has infested this place," I said slowly. "The entire convent has become a conduit for an entity."

I knew it to be true. I could feel those eyes watching me still from the shadows, as if the building itself were watching me from every angle, and I could feel the blood of the entity flowing through the air...

It was such a difficult sensation to describe, a feeling which rests wholly in the spiritual and not the physical, but I knew, I simply *knew*, just as one might sense when being watched from behind, that we were not alone in this place.

Archie stared at me for a moment, clearly uncertain of exactly what to think. Truth be told, I wasn't quite sure what to think either. All these strange sensations, I was somewhat familiar with them from my past experiences aiding Father Martin, but... ideas were beginning to form in my mind of what was going on, like disparate pieces of a jigsaw puzzle, but I had no view yet of what image was forming.

"Show me around," I invited Archie. "Please."

He nodded slowly and together we began to traipse around the old halls of the convent, our boots making terrible echoes as they banged against the solid stone floor. The entire building was freezing, immeasurably colder than the already icy outside air had been. The roof was missing, but even so... the building should have at the very least been as cold as outside if not warmer, not so much icier, and the longer we spent in the ruins, the more I began to detect a strange odour, like spoiled meat.

It was as though somebody had left a cart full of dead fish to rot in the sun for a week before dispersing the ripe carcasses throughout the building. The smell wasn't overwhelming, but it was truly repulsive; a faint smell but the most noisome, nauseating odour I had ever encountered despite its mildness.

49

I had, however, come across that smell before, and I knew exactly what it meant. I still needed to gather more information before I could make any definitive decisions, but this was a strong sign.

We wandered through the ruins a while, encircling the cloisters and stopping by the altar. We peaked into what remained of the various lodgings and chambers of the nuns, and eventually found our way back to the front door.

All the time, as we walked around, I had felt eyes staring at me in the darkness, and sensed another presence, as though there were three of us wandering through those ruins rather than two. Often, I saw a silhouette in the corner of my eye, as though a third person walked behind me, just out of sight, but whenever I turned to look... the shadows were empty.

Sometimes, in the quiet moments, I thought I heard hushed voices whispering in the darkness too, as if empty rooms in fact were inhabited by two or three invisible people who spoke in hushed tones as we approached, but fell silent as we entered the room. I never caught what they said, and indeed I'm not sure that I would have understood it even if I had heard any words in their chattering.

Archie, it seemed, was more or less oblivious to these things. I think he sensed that something was wrong with that place, but that may well have simply been that the atmosphere was one of eerie and unsettling dread and darkness.

"Well?" Archie asked as we stopped once more in the front door.

"This is no longer a house of God. These ruins are home to a far more sinister entity. This convent has an insidious squatter," I told Archie gravely. I was certain now of what resided within that place, but still did not know why Sister Myrtle had summoned it, if indeed she had intentionally brought the thing into our world. The picture was becoming clear, but I had not yet completed the puzzle.

By now it must have been almost midnight, but I insisted to Archie that he show me Sister Myrtle's laboratory. Eventually, begrudgingly, he agreed, and led me down a dark, shadowy corridor and through an archway. Ahead were a series of steps winding down into the darkness, into the old crypts of the convent.

Archie stood at the top of the stairs and gestured for me to go ahead.

"You're not coming?" I asked him.

He simply shook his head.

"But we only have one lantern," I reasoned.

He passed it to me. "I'd rather wait up here, alone in the dark, than go down there."

I frowned. "Archie, why not? What's down there?"

He just shook his head. "Nothing. I don't know, but it's not about what's down there now. It's about what *was* down there. Four years ago. All that's left are memories, but I don't want to remember that place."

I just nodded slowly. I wanted to ask more, but I'd already retraumatised the poor boy with my questions enough times that night. So, I took the lantern and I descended into the crypts beneath the convent.

Stone archways marched off ahead of me, with more archways leading off to either side, like a grid. Random archways were filled in with solid stone walls, sometimes making a room but not always, and all in all the place was like a maze. It was difficult to navigate down there in the dim, flickering light of the lantern. Shadows seemed to crawl and dance upon the walls, making unnatural, unholy shapes which seemed to leer and grimace at me.

Still, I felt those eyes staring at me, but now the sensation was less like a group staring at me from up ahead, and more as though I were in the midst of the crowd. Now, the eyes watched me from every direction, but there was a violating presence to their stares, a discomfort, as though that which watched me was stood right beside me, as though their presences were touching me, pressed against my body.

51

My skin crawled at that thought and I shivered, not from the freezing cold, but with discomfort. Down here, the place was somehow even colder still, impossibly more freezing than the outside world or the ruins above. Again, I saw silhouettes of figures standing in the darkness, just out the corner of my eye and yet when I looked... I was alone in the dark.

There was whispering too, quiet, hushed voices, whispering nonsensically in the crypts, saying no words that I understood. I followed the sounds of the whispering, and was led ever deeper into the catacombs, straying further and further into the vault beneath the convent. Up ahead, through the darkness, I saw a doorway into a chamber, the stone here deformed and cracked, as though the fire had been hotter here than anywhere else.

Sister Myrtle's laboratory.

I went inside, and found myself in a relatively large chamber filled with wooden tables and desks and drawers and similar such furnishings. There were, or there had been, dozens of books and notes and glass bottles and vials all around the room, on every table and shelf, but... the fire had shattered and melted the glass and burned the books. Most of the paper was nothing but ash, but a few crinkled, dry pages remained of a few of the books.

The air was colder here than anywhere else in the ruins, and thicker too. That same sensation I had felt upon entering the convent, the feeling of a presence spread thin through the air... it was thicker here than anywhere else.

The whispering had fallen silent as soon as I entered the room, but now it was like the entire crowd of silent, invisible watchers were pressed against me, choking me. I felt a horrible, oppressive presence bearing down upon me, like a great, ancient and powerful force were gazing into my very soul, judging me.

I wandered around the laboratory for a bit, examining some of the ruined remains of the books and notes. On one table there were a few scraps of paper which had just about survived the fires, though they had been crinkled and dried and turned as brittle as dust by the heat and smoke, and soot was painted over a lot of their surfaces.

Very, *very* gingerly, I picked up the notes and began examining them, reading them in the light of my lantern. It seemed to have been a sort of diary that Sister Myrtle had kept, just a few jotted-down entries in the days leading up to the fire. This was the final, damning piece of evidence which proved to me unequivocally that Sister Myrtle had indeed summoned something from Hell intentionally, and exactly what she had summoned. I will never forget what those pages said...

***

13th May 1947

Tonight, my friends, I believe I have found, at last, the final piece of the inscription. For centuries we have searched through manuscripts and documents in search of truth and now, at last, I have found it.

The Book of Kazzkhan's missing pages, which we have hunted for since our order was founded, at last I have discovered what is written upon them. I have found the ingredients needed to complete the ritual, and I have every confidence that I will be successful in completing the summoning.

Fear not, my sisters. Our time has come.

Many of the ingredients were not hard to come by. Sage, basil and thyme I was able to procure from Sister Andrea's herb garden and the garlic and ginger were easy to come across in the market in Ashton.

The other ingredients; the blood of a woman's time of month, the semen of a virgin man and the bones of a stillborn wolf... these may be harder to produce. The monthly blood I can source myself, by fortune my time is approaching in the coming days, but the semen and bones I will have to think on carefully. As for the vessel... the scripture specifies very carefully what is needed. This will not be easy to find.

15th May 1947

I have almost everything. Quite by luck alone, my time began this morning and so I already was able to collect the sixth ingredient of a woman's monthly blood. The semen I was also able to find thanks to a rather disgraceful deal with a young gentleman from Ashton village, and the eighth ingredient... this I must still think on carefully. It will be hard to safely come across such bones. As for the vessel... I still haven't the faintest idea how to procure such a thing.

I pray now to Kazzkhan, to our master who art in Hell, harrowed be thy name, to deliver these final ingredients unto us such that thou

54

might walk the Earth alongside us, as master and slaves. I give myself to you, my lord.

16ᵗʰ May 1947

Success, at last! In exchange for a golden chalice lifted from the convent's wine cellar, I was able to purchase the services and silence of a local hunter from the village, and he was able to find and slay a pregnant wolf, whose child I was able to pull from the mother's womb. The process was gruelling work, but I now have extracted the bones of the stillborn wolf cub. Only the vessel remained, but at last Kazzkhan heard my prayers. Today, not three hours ago, a young woman who had brought shame upon her house came to us in seek of guidance and help in delivering the baby she had given herself in shame and sin. Mother Superior volunteered to watch the babe while the mother rested at home in the village, but it was not difficult to slip a little laudanum in her wine and take the babe for myself.

At last, the ingredients are ready and the vessel is mine. My lord, my love, Kazzkhan, tonight, I summon you.

***

I read those words alone in the dark on burnt paper in the dim light of Archie's lantern in the crypt beneath the burnt-down ruins of St. Agnes Convent, Inverness, and as I read those words I wept and I prayed.

I prayed for the soul of that innocent infant whom Sister Myrtle had stolen, and for the young mother whose child had been lost to her. I prayed for the souls of the other nuns in the convent, for the twenty-four innocent women of Christ who had died in those flames, and for the two survivors; Sister Bathsheba and Sister Clementina, who would, I was sure, be plagued by nightmares and suffering for the rest of their lives.

I prayed for the foolish hunter and the young man from the village who had unknowingly been accomplices to the wicked nun who had abandoned God and committed a vile act of sacrilege and evil.

I stood there a moment and wept, an overwhelming sadness gripping my soul as the very thought of all the evil and all the sin that had come to be in that very room washed over me and left its mark on my very soul.

As I sit here now, on the eve of June in 2021, seventy years later... I am weeping as I write this. After all this time... after all these decades, I have never before told anybody what I read on those pages. I have never before told anybody what that evil woman had to do to summon that thing from Hell.

A real woman did those things, took those things... she really summoned something from Hell, and it really required her to complete such horrible acts, such vile and offensive sins.

I knew now what she had summoned, and I knew now how she had done it. All I needed was to know why. I needed to learn more about this entity and then... then I could combat it. But not there. Not then.

I needed to leave, to return to Ashton and my room in The Bloody Stallion and to my books.

I had seen enough of those ruins for a lifetime.

And that's when I suddenly noticed it.

I think I had been aware of it for a little while, but it wasn't until just then that I became fully aware that I was not alone in the room.

Out of the corner of my eye... a figure was stood behind me, in the doorway to the lab.

I turned suddenly, trying to get a glimpse of the figure, half expecting it to vanish like all the others had, but it didn't.

There, stood in the doorway, meeting my gaze, was another nun like myself. She wore a white and pale blue habit, and she sort of hunched over forwards, slumping a little. Her eyes were completely white, without pupils or irises, as though they'd rolled up in their sockets, and her mouth was caked in blood, an unsettling grin spread ear-to-ear with crimson bloodstained teeth on show. The grin was too wide, unnaturally wide, stretched out so wide that it almost looked like a grimace of pain more than anything else.

I was frozen on the spot, staring at this strange nun who, despite her lack of pupils, still met my gaze. I don't know how I could tell she was staring back at me, but she was. She just was.

She began to drift backwards, gliding into the shadows smoothly, as though she had wheels and not feet. I came forwards, bringing the lantern with me but leaving those papers behind on the desk, ensuring that I kept the nun within the dim sphere of light which was centred upon the lantern.

The nun only went backwards a yard or so, enough to let me out the doorway, before stopping, still staring at me. Without moving, she raised her arm – a sudden, jerking sort of motion that wasn't a motion at all, her arm simply was raised one moment when it hadn't been before – and pointed down the passageway. I came out of the laboratory and peered into the darkness, but the passageway disappeared into shadow away from the lantern.

"Who are you?" I asked the nun.

She did not reply, did not move, did not say or do anything. She was, I suddenly realised, not even breathing.

This was not a real person, not anymore. At the very least, this was an apparition of a memory. It was certainly not a living thing.

I stared down the hall again, moving my attention away from this strange spirit, and began to slowly make my way along the corridor. I suddenly came to a stop when I saw that, up ahead, the passage terminated in a solid stone wall with no way forward. A dead end.

I turned back and went the way I had come. I'd only gone a few yards, been gone a few seconds, and the footsteps echoed throughout the crypt and yet, silently, as if she had never been there, the nun was gone.

I decided at that point that I'd had quite enough of that place and practically ran for the stairs, not a very dignified action for a nun, I confess, but I was – quite understandably – scared sockless! I ran all the way to the stairs and came up them as fast as I could, quite breathless by the time I reached Archie, sitting at the top of the steps, waiting for me quite patiently.

"You alright?" he asked me, dreadfully confused. "What happened?"

I took a moment to catch my breath. "I'll explain... later... for now... back to the pub..."

I suddenly realised that I hadn't eaten since I'd had a small and disappointing meal on the train the previous morning and I was rather hungry.

"I need some dinner," I told him, still catching my breath.

Archie nodded and smiled. "We can sort that out, no problem."

The trip back down the hill was fairly pleasant, and indeed the air seemed to be a sauna as far as I was concerned, compared with the freezing icy cold of Sister Myrtle's laboratory. I had no doubts now as to what was in that place... all the signs were there and based on the ingredients for Myrtle's ritual... I knew precisely what had been summoned, though the reasons were still not entirely clear. Now I could dig through my many books and the Biblical scriptures and piece together exactly what I ought to do about it.

The wind died down fairly quickly after we left the convent and the further we strayed from the ruins, the fewer eyes seemed to watch us from the darkness. Archie's shotgun never came in handy and we never saw any bears, but it made me feel safer to have both the gun and its wielder for company.

Eventually we made it back to Ashton and Archie took me discretely through the back alleys and hidden streets of the village back to The Bloody Stallion. After spending an hour coming back down the hill it was after half-past-one when we finally made it back to the inn, and the place was completely deserted; closed for the night.

"What can I get you to eat?" Archie asked, going round the back of the bar and towards the kitchen.

"Oh, I don't know. Whatever is easiest for you, I'm not a fussy eater," I told him sweetly, though I admit I was still a little shaken after my ordeal in the crypts of the convent.

I sat down on a stool by the bar again and began to converse with Archie as he began to cook.

"So," he began. "What's the verdict on that place?"

I took a deep breath.

"I know what's in that convent, I know who brought it there and, once I've had a look through my books, I'll know how to get rid of it. I don't know what happened to those poor priests or why it was put there, but I can only hope that these things will become clear upon further investigation," I explained slowly.

"And what's up there?" he asked from the kitchen.

"A Demon."

Chapter 4: The Shadows of The Town

"A Demon?" Archie asked, clearly more than a little confused.

I just nodded gravely, my mind somewhat overflowing with different thoughts and feelings about what I'd experienced in those ruins.

"What's a Demon?" he asked. "I mean I've heard of them but... what *are* they?"

Behind the bar was a hatch in the wall, through which I could see the kitchen, making our conversation a little easier, though I confess the distance combined with the sounds of food sizzling in a frying pan made talk more difficult.

I sighed and paused a moment as I pondered how I might answer such a question.

"I'll give you the same long-winded, roundabout sort of answer that my mentor gave me when I put to him that same question, and indeed it was the same answer his mentor gave him when he asked," I began. "A person isn't just a block of meat that can think. A person is a soul. A spirit... ideas, thoughts, feelings, memories, emotions, sensations, joy, hate, love, pain, opinions, political viewpoints, ideologies, personal beliefs... all these things, they are not defined by a physical form and yet they make up the identity of a person, the most important piece, these things *are* the person. The body is just a package, a box containing a soul of gold and silver and jewels. A person is a puppeteer with a puppet of flesh and blood and bone. When a person passes away, their body and soul are separated permanently, the puppet is taken from the puppeteer and buried in the ground to rot or burned to ash and scattered, but the soul lives on, the person, the identity, this continues."

He nodded, I think understanding well what I was saying but not yet appreciating its relevance.

"Now, every soul is, at the dawn of life, a blank slate without character or personality or identity. A new-born baby has a soul but they are hardly a functioning person, hardly an individual. Throughout life, many people are subjected to horrors, dark horrors, terrible things that one should not like to dwell on, and it can scar the soul. It can teach a person lessons that they never wanted to learn. The soul is the heart and the mind, and these things can be broken and injured, never slain, but injured. Scarred," I continued.

I took a moment to pause, recalling my mentor's words.

"If a person is scarred in life and rendered incapable of believing in love or left in a state of perpetual hollowness, these scars cannot be healed. If life cannot heal a wound, then neither can death. These people, these souls, are left wanting, yearning for something which only life can give except now it is too late, and so these people remain on this Earth, trapped in a state of lovelessness, knowing only hate and fear and pain. We call these people ghosts, we call them phantoms and spectres and vengeful spirits, but in truth they are just people, trapped in pain," I paused once more, preparing myself for the crux of this description.

"Now consider an Angel," I continued. "An Angel has no flesh, their bodies are made from divinity and thunder and fire. An Angel has no blood, instead their hearts are filled with love and kindness and warmth. An Angel has no bones, instead their beings are held together and kept upright by strong faith, by passion, and by courage. Suppose now that an Angel dies. Not only that, but an Angel commits ritualistic suicide, sacrificing themself to curse a God they have forgotten to love. Their body is separated from their identity forever and destroyed. Divinity and power, love and kindness, faith and passion... gone. Forever. An Angel, a creature of such spiritual might that they could inhabit Heaven alongside God himself, a creature so righteous that even though they have freewill they have never, in all of eternity, never once sinned... imagine that creature commits sinful, cultic suicide and renders itself into a creature of hate, of malice, an ancient being of light now mutated into a dark creature of death which has forgotten how to love, and forgotten how to feel joy. Suppose this suicidal spirit were then cast from Heaven for its crimes and banished to Hell, banished to the pit. That is a Demon. A creature older than time who once was like God, but chose to commit a sinful suicide

61

as an act of defiance and hatred to spit in the face of God, damned to Hell forever. A creature of hate and malice, one who no longer understands love, one who can never be bargained with or reasoned with or bartered with, one who feels nothing but pain and wants nothing more than to lash out at creation and the God who built it. That is a Demon."

Archie stared at me in silence for a moment, I think trying to comprehend what that might mean, trying his best to appreciate the gravity and magnitude of such things, trying his best to wrap his tiny mortal mind around the divinity of the infinite and wretchedness of the unholy. That feat, that understanding... that is something I am still yet to achieve. Even now, after so many decades of work, even now I think I shall never understand. Not in this life at least.

"What do they do when they come here... to our world I mean?" he asked. He was nervous to ask that question, I could tell, as if he were afraid that if I answered it, my words may bite him.

"They want to attack God and that which he has made," I replied rather bluntly. "They are spirits of hate and they want to take power and to corrupt those who are made and loved by God. Namely, us. Humanity. Ultimately, Demons want to insult God, and to do so they want to twist and break us, to make our souls like them, and to... consume us. Demons want souls. Human souls. They cannot just take one, however, you have to offer up your soul. And the best way to make a person give up their soul... torture them and convince them that the only way to make it stop is to give in. Possession is difficult, but it will only give the Demon a body. Those are easy to manipulate, we do it all day every day without even noticing. Once it has achieved possession, however, that's when the real work begins for the Demon. By that point, an exorcism is vital, because if a possessed person is not interfered with, the Demon *will* break them and it *will* take their soul. We are only Human and they... they used to be Angels."

From then on, for a while, I sat in ominous silence as Archie cooked in the kitchen.

62

After perhaps ten more minutes, Archie came back with two plates of food; bacon, eggs, sausages, some strange mixture of potatoes and onions and another odd, square, flatter sort of sausage. All of it had been made in a frying pan, and seemed to have been rather burned on the outside, though I only learnt later that this was the intention and that Archie was, in fact, a skilled cook. He was just Scottish.

"Dig in," he instructed sweetly as he set one plate before me alongside a knife and fork, and set the other in front of himself.

"Thank you," I smiled to him kindly.

"So... you think there's a Demon... a dead angry Angel... up in the convent?" he asked me through a mouthful of bacon.

I nodded, and unlike the Scotsman waited until after I'd finished my mouthful to speak. "Yes. I found some diary entries from Sister Myrtle in the ruins of her laboratory. It was clear she was working with other people and attempting to summon a Demon called Kazzkhan. It seemed they were using a grimoire – a book of magic – written exclusively about this Demonic entity, in order to attempt to reconstruct a ritual to summon it from Hell. There are all manner of sinful, evil, wicked practises that can be used to commune with or even summon satanic forces, but I've never come across one so... grotesque. For some reason, Sister Myrtle and some other group of people seemed to be desperate to reach out to this Demon in particular, and four years ago... she succeeded. I don't know why, but that isn't strictly relevant. The good news is that I've now verified exactly what I am up against and I know for a fact it is still in the ruins of the convent. Spiritual entities are often bound to certain objects or locations unless they can possess a living host, and it seems this entity is bound to the ruins."

Archie nodded slowly. If even half of that went in his head I'd have been impressed, I certainly hadn't understood any of it the first time I'd been told all that in my training.

"How do you know it's a Demon?" he asked, again with a mouth full of food.

"Several things gave it away. There are certain... Demonic signs... which can hint at what might truly be going on. First of all, there was the smell of rotting meat throughout the convent. Rancid smells are useful for determining the difference between Human and Demonic spirits. How cold that place was... that gave me a hint too. Then there was Sister Myrtle's diary and the ingredients used for the ritual... such terrible deeds are not necessary to just summon a ghost. Things such as these," I explained slowly, listing off the few signs of many which were at the top of my head.

"Demonic signs...," Archie mused for a moment. "Demonic signs... you know... I think I might have seen a few of them myself..."

"Pray tell?" I invited.

"Well... I told you about the miscarriages... there's also... well I don't know if it's connected because this was going on since way before the convent burned down...," he began with terrible uncertainty.

"It's possible Sister Myrtle had made multiple attempts to summon the Demon. Just invoking it could easily be enough to cause some... odd events...," I explained, reassuring the boy that he was no fool.

"Right, well then...," he continued, taking a deep breath. "You've noticed the thunder, I'm sure, but there's never any lightning. Since the place burned down we've usually just had storms here, storms with thunder and no lightning, but before... well... one day it was a clear sky, blue as blue can be, sun shining down on us and all... and five minutes later the sky was black like the middle of the night but... no stars... and there was thunder and lightning and hail... it hailed balls of ice as big as my eyes... sometimes as big as my fist... and the rain too... the rain came down like Noah's flood and left us with half our roads covered in mud... then, five minutes later, the sky was clear again and the ice was already melted. Then it happened again, a week later, then a few days after that... eventually it was happening twice a day, seven days a week, then thrice a day... and then the convent burned down. And, a few years earlier than all that... back in... thirty-something... '39 maybe... or '38... but every animal in the village... all of them... every animal in the whole village… every dog, every cat, every goat and sheep and donkey and rat and cow and pig… every animal in the whole village dropped dead at once. The birds just dropped out of the sky and two or three hundred fish came floating up to the surface of the loch. It was like they'd rehearsed it, I mean it, all at once, all in the exact same second I reckon, they all just keeled over, dead as a door nail. The doctors and vets and all… they couldn't explain it. Heart attacks or brain bleeds they said but… they had no idea how it had all happened at once."

Archie took a pause for breath, having had to fight himself somewhat to get all that off his chest. I sensed that these were things he'd had dark thoughts on for some time, but I recalled him mentioning that the village didn't talk about what they all knew to be true.

I just nodded for a while and ate as I listened to Archie's words. It all made perfect sense. The storms, the hail, the lightning-less thunderstorms… these were far less common but certainly they were tell-tale signs of Demonic activity. The animal deaths were important signs too, though I had never before heard of it on such a large scale, or of it happening all at once. These things did not prove to me that I was facing a Demonic entity, that I already knew, but Archie's tale certainly gave me a perspective of the scale of power against which I now was faced.

"It feels good to finally talk to somebody about that. For years… we've all just pretended like there was nothing happening. This whole village is insane," Archie grumbled.

I just shook my head and smiled sympathetically. "They're afraid, and when faced with overwhelming fear of something we do not understand, we are all prone to making foolish decisions. I cannot blame your neighbours for choosing to ignore these things. They cannot do anything about it, so why should they try and do anything? At least if they ignore it, they can maintain some normalcy. That's not to say that your frustrations are unjustified, however, I think it's perfectly reasonable to be upset with them for this."

Archie shrugged, clearly in no mood to be quite so sympathetic to the people he was forced to live near.

"How does summoning a Demon work then?" he asked after a moment, clearly wanting to change the subject.

I recalled Father Martin's answer to that very same question when I had asked it.

"God's creation is like an ocean. Here, we drift on little dinghies in the surface waters, basking in the sunlight of Heaven. The deeper one goes, the darker it gets. Hell is at the very bottom. Demons want to come to the surface, to find all our little dinghies and claim them as their own, here the dinghies represent our mortal bodies. Summoning a Demon is like throwing a weighted rope ladder down to the depths of Hell so that a Demon can climb up, sometimes with a specific entity in mind, but not always," I explained, recalling the same words Father Martin had told me.

I realised that many of the explanations I was giving to Archie were, verbatim, identical to the explanations my mentor had given to me. Looking back on it all now, I recognise this as evidence I was living through borrowed faith, trusting in scripture and holy practise because it had come to me through Father Martin, rather than trusting in our works because it had come from God.

Archie nodded, the oceanic explanation seeming to resonate with him well. I wondered if that was because of his life growing up on the shores of Loch Ashie. Either way, that seemed to be the first of my teachings which he had fully understood, something I took as a sign I was improving in my understanding of the boy and the village as a whole.

Archie mused on that for a moment, digesting my lessons as he digested his crispy Scottish food.

We both finished our meals and then, not a moment after he had swallowed his last bite, he posed me a question I don't think I shall ever forget.

66

"In your ocean and dinghies metaphor... I guess breaking a dinghy is dying, and a Demon hijacking a dinghy would be like getting possessed... so can a Demon hijack the dinghy and then push the person that's meant to be there overboard?" he asked thoughtfully.

I hadn't been ready for such a philosophical question from a boy who had seemed, until now at least, to be sweet enough but not particularly bright. I had no answer to that and, I realised some time after, it was because it was not a question I had ever thought to ask myself. I only knew what Father Martin had told me.

I tried to think for a moment what that might mean, if a Demon could possess a person and then, without killing the body, prise flesh from spirit and command a living vessel as though it were the Demon's own.

In truth, I did not know, and though I spent a great deal of time thinking upon that question both that night and for quite some time to come, it was never one I was able to answer on my own.

"That's a very good question. I shouldn't think so, no. In order to separate the soul and body, one must kill the body and thus sink the dinghy," I told Archie, making up an answer on the spot, but I confess... even as I said it, I doubted myself.

I've always regretted the way I answered that question. I was being arrogant and showing off. I had no idea what the truth was, but I wanted Archie to trust my judgement and have faith in me to get the job done and in doing so I failed him and I acted in poor judgement.

I should simply have told him I did not know. I am mortal, I cannot know all the secrets of the cosmos, especially when I was only twenty-six! We Humans are capable of asking infinitely more questions than we can answer, but I was guilty, in that moment, of pride and though I may not exactly have lied to the boy, I gave him my best guess, I deceived him by intention; I made him believe I was a far more confident and skilled investigator than in truth I was.

67

I have carried that guilt with me for seventy years, and I know it's foolish and a little silly, I didn't *really* do anything wrong, it was no big deal, but... it was one example among many of my pride. I have felt embarrassed by that flaw for a long time and it feels good to finally confess that sin, here in writing, and to let it go.

Perhaps that is why I am writing this book. I started it as therapy, to move past the traumatic memories under the advice of my oldest and closest friend, Jules, but now... perhaps this is about more than just my trauma. Perhaps this book might act as a form of confession, such that I might be absolved of my sins at long last.

I digress, and return to the story.

Archie and I talked a little while longer, but I could tell the young man was rapidly losing his focus and I realised it was nearing three in the morning. I instructed him quite sternly to go to bed at once and bid him goodnight, creeping up the stairs as slowly as I could until finally reaching my breezy little attic room.

I closed and locked the door, before sitting down on the edge of my bed and praying.

"Good evening, God. Or... morning perhaps... I am anxious once more, my God. I believe I know what lies in that convent... I thank you for your protection over Archie and I as we explored those ruins... and I pray for strength to stomach what I saw written down on those pages of Sister Myrtle's diary... such sinful acts, my God... I pray for the souls of the innocent nuns who perished in that fire, and for your peace upon the infant who died unfairly by that vile woman's hands. I pray for the mother of that child, my God, and I pray too for relief upon the minds of the nuns who fled that inferno, I pray for your love and wisdom to shower upon them like warm rains," I prayed aloud, mumbling out my little soliloquy to the Almighty.

I paused and took a breath.

I realised I was letting my anxiety turn to anger and tried to calm myself.

I closed my eyes and reminded myself of my vows and of my devotion to holiness and purity. "I pray too for Sister Myrtle, God. She was only Human and she was clearly deceived by a Demon. I know all too well that those fiends feed on pain and uncertainty and to be implicated as she was, that girl must have been full of both, and so I pray for her soul, Lord. Every Human being, no matter how misguided, is one of your beloved creations and I pray God that perhaps repentance was within her as her final breath left her body, and I pray that in your almighty wisdom and justice and forgiveness that she is at peace now, graced with your salvation and wrapped in your peace forevermore."

I took a breath and gave myself a moment to think, a moment to simply be in peace with my creator. I have always felt that forgiveness and love are warmer, kinder colours to wear than hatred or judgement. I knew nothing about that nun's life. I knew nothing of the contents of her soul. Who was I to say she was wicked or evil? She had made evil choices, yes, but have we not all?

One thing which I thought then which has stuck with me even now, a thought which came to my mind in that quiet moment of prayer, was that we are all Human. Good actions do not make us good people and sinful actions do not make us evil people. We do not alternate between being good people and evil people on different days, we simply are at all times just people; flawed and sinful but still just trying our best. The alternation between good and evil is a basic component of our very nature.

Perhaps it is simply that I am too old, and I've seen both more good and, equally, more evil than most people ever dream of... perhaps I'm just a mad old fool... but to be Human is to walk the line between God and Satan and pick a side. The Devil and Hell's Demons abandoned God and chose evil long ago, while Heaven's Angels are faithful in the creator to the end, but we mortals with our short lives and our powerless, painful little existences... we must pick a side.

One is not evil for falling down, nor is one inherently good for climbing up. We are all created equal by God and created to be made in God's image, thus

69

we all are simply Human. We are not defined by our choices, perhaps, but by our intentions. We do not see the scope of creation and we rarely can know for certain how the consequences of our actions will unfold. It is our intentions alone which may define us, for what mortal believes and intends and revels in being evil?

Are we not all trying our best?

These thoughts, this great philosophy I suppose... it all sort of bubbled up in my mind in one go, erupting forth in a series of partially formed, malnourished concepts which slowly fused together into a series of ideas which I found myself overwhelmed by. I was, most certainly, taken aback by these thoughts which had, as far as I was concerned, come more or less from nowhere within my own mind, but, I decided, instead had come from God.

I sat back and let those thoughts dwell within me for some time before I felt able to form thoughts and prayers again.

"Thank you, God, for that insight. I praise your infinite wisdom, my God. Sister Myrtle was doing her best, I am sure, and however misguided her actions were, I hold no doubt that her intentions were pure. I pray for her soul, my God, I pray she might have witnessed the error of her ways and come to find your love before it was too late," I prayed once more, feeling within me a holiness and wholesomeness which I can only describe as the opposite of the sensation which those ruins gave me and a sensation which filled me from within my soul, rather than assaulting me from the outside world. "Thank you for your love, God. I pray now for your wisdom, that I might discern precisely what to do in my combat with the fiendish entity in those ruins. In the name of Jesus Christ I pray, amen."

I took another breath and permitted myself a quiet moment of peace, before standing. It was still only the very early hours of the morning now, and yet I found myself in a position of being entirely wide awake, devoid of fatigue or exhaustion. I had, of course, slept all day, and so now, in the night, came my time to act.

I stretched out my arms and legs and gave my limbs a little shake to prepare myself for what was to come.

I sat at the desk and began trawling through the books of scripture and demonology which I had brought, my mind open to God's voice as I prepared myself for what was to come.

I did not know the details of it, but I suspected now that Kazzkhan had murdered the seven priests which had come before me. It would surely murder me as well. I prayed that I might be the one who could save the town. I of course prayed for my own survival – a prayer which, you may have noticed by way of the fact I am still alive, seventy years later, was answered – but my priority was not my life. I had given my life and soul up to God a long time ago. The people of Ashton were my priority. I was here to save them. I prayed that I would succeed where the other priests had failed, no matter what it might cost me.

Saving that town... it did not cost me my life in the end, but... when eventually I did leave that place, I was not the same nun who rode in on the back of an applecart.

Chapter 5: The Memory of a Conjuring

For what remained of the night and indeed for much of the following day, I did not sleep and I confess I barely moved other than to make use of the toilet or to get the occasional glass of water and a small meal from Archie at the bar.

Whenever I would go downstairs for these things, the young Scotsman would ask me how my research was going, to which I would often answer that I was close to being prepared. Yet no matter how much I read, I found that I was never close enough.

The books I read discussed exorcism and demonology, they examined the functions of our practises and gave many verses of scripture and prayers to cite when facing dark entities. They also told of old lore and histories; litanies of the intersection between our world and the Demonic, and altogether told a fairly frightful narrative of all manner of cults and witches and dark acts and evil deeds. All night and for most of the day, I read through these tomes, desperate to find some information on the entity known as Kazzkhan, the fiend which had taken up residence in the ruins of the convent, and yet whenever I began to think I had discovered something important, the investigations only led me to footnotes which cited a volume titled "The Book of Kazzkhan". This was, I recalled, the volume which Sister Myrtle had referred to in the notes I had found in her laboratory, but which I sadly did not possess, and if it had been in her possession on the night of the fire... then by now the book surely was just ash.

I sighed, growing ever more exasperated.

I knew that a Demon resided in the ruins of the convent, I knew its name, I knew that it had been summoned, I knew the ingredients that had been used to conjure it, and I knew who had performed the ritual. I could gather from the Demonic signs which it influenced and by the atrocities committed in order to call it forth that this was a particularly powerful entity, but this information was useless if I could not use it.

This was a powerful Demon and so driving it from the convent would be difficult. This was not some malicious entity randomly selecting a victim to possess, to cling to like a leech, this was an extraordinarily influential being which had been dragged up from Hell itself, which had caused catastrophic signs and which, it seemed, was bound to the ruins of the convent. It had already overpowered seven priests who each had far more experience and wisdom than I did, and it had been specifically selected to be summoned, presumably for a specific purpose, though I knew not what this purpose might be.

Combatting such an entity would take more than just an exorcism delivered by the village priest, this would require dedication and a more directed assault. I needed data, I needed to know exactly how this Demon operated, I needed to know exactly what prayers to cite in the face of this adversary. And yet this Demon seemed to be nothing more than a footnote, with a book which I could learn nothing about.

My research was not going well. I was perpetually close to finding the information I needed and yet I was never successful.

At around two in the afternoon, I decided to take a rest and let my subconscious mind reflect upon my research while I slept, and so I made some brief prayers for guidance and went down for a nap.

No sooner had I closed my eyes than I suddenly felt a hand wrap around my throat.

I sat up straight, startled, and shouted with a jump, but this time... this time the hand didn't let go.

A long, gnarled, twisted hand with flesh that alternated between raw, vulnerable patches of pink sinew and dark, burnt regions of charred flesh, had extended out from the shadows in the far corner of the room, which suddenly seemed far darker than it had any right being, and gripped my neck tight. The arm was unnaturally long, just as burnt and crooked as the hand at its end, and seemed to have been stretched, twisted and broken until it was seven feet long, reaching out from the darkness.

Suddenly, the arm pulled and I was sent hurtling towards the corner of the room.

I fell into the shadows and suddenly I seemed to be in a place of nothing but darkness and death. A moment later I returned from this void into our world once more, but now I was in Sister Myrtle's laboratory.

Not the ruins of the laboratory.

The door here had not been disintegrated to ash, the stone had not been blackened by soot and smoke, the books and notes and glass vials had not been destroyed. And there, stood in the centre of the room, busying herself with half a dozen different items, was the same nun I had seen in the present day in the ruins of the laboratory.

Her eyes were not pure white now, but sparkling blue, her teeth were white, not bloodstained crimson, and her mouth did not stretch out into an unnatural ear-to-ear grin, but was pursed in frustration as she performed some sort of chemical experiments, mixing different fluids and herbs together in glass vials.

I could only presume that this was Sister Myrtle.

I took all of this in after being in the room less than a second and, of course, my hands naturally flew to my throat, of which the unnatural hand had now let go.

Even then, even as I stood there, I knew that what I saw was a dream. I knew that I was asleep, safe in my bed in The Bloody Stallion. I knew that I was dreaming.

And yet...

I also knew this was real.

What I saw was no normal dream, but an illusion. The grotesque hand which had summoned me to this place, to this memory, had rather given it away. The Demon was showing me this, though I didn't know why.

But, I knew I was not really there, and I knew that I was safe.

And that only fuelled my pride.

I was safe and so I threw caution to the wind.

I began exploring the laboratory, looking for anything that might help. If there were any books that might help me understand how to combat this Demon, they would certainly be there, in that laboratory, ruined by the fire in the real world, but in that memory from before the destruction of the convent...

I trawled through the books on the shelf, seemingly invisible to the nun as she worked, but entirely capable – thankfully – of interacting with the volumes in her possession.

There, laying open upon the table, was an ancient text, the pages of which were filled with strange and uncomfortable diagrams of creatures which seemed neither animal, nor Human, but somewhere in between.

One such creature was like a serpent with the face of a man and the wings of a bat, another was like a naked man with the feet and horns of a goat and an upside down cross carved into his flesh.

There were other creatures depicted too, things that grew ever more explicit and unholy, carved with more and more vulgar symbols and each with less and less dignity, exposing more of themselves and seeming to perform disgraceful acts. The most despicable of these must have been a creature in the shape of a down-facing five-pointed star, its two up-facing parts being the upper halves of a man and a woman, each naked and with all manner of harsh diagrams and symbols carved bloodily into their uncovered flesh.

Their cheeks had been sliced open to stretch out their mouths into wicked grins and their ears were long and pointed. Curved horns like those of a ram protruded from their foreheads, leaving blood spilling from the skin where the horns had pierced their flesh. Their eyes were completely black and tears of blood spilled down their cheeks.

Two of the lower three points of their star-like form were each parts of a different animal. The left-hand lower section of this grotesque form was the backend and legs of a goat, with cloven hooves and shaggy fur which was matted with blood and black oil, while the right-hand lower section was the tail of a serpent, again spattered in blood and carved with all manner of unholy and sacrilegious symbols.

These four components joined together at the hips of the man and woman, forming a grotesque and unsettling sort of four-way pelvis, at the base of which was a rotting, festering, maggot-infected orifice, through which was passing the central lower component of this fiend's form.

It was like a birth, except childbirth is a holy miracle and this... this was anything but holy.

Firstly, the main shape of this thing was like a man, but horrifically scarred and burnt, and rotted away as though it had been buried for decades. The creature had wings too, black wings like a bat, wings full of holes and made from smoke and Hellfire. The thing was covered in eyes too, each of them blind; milky and sightless orbs which protruded from sockets all over the flesh of the creature. It had horns too, curved ram horns which violently exploded from inside its skull as that of the man and woman above had, and these horns were drenched in blood. The creature had the legs of a goat too, with black, blood-matted fur that scarcely covered many more blind eyes, and this monster's open mouth revealed great fangs, like those of a serpent.

This creature passed through the orifice at the base of the larger one, composing its fifth and final section and together making a single grotesque fiend.

All of these fiends had names given beneath them, all of them given roles and titles and descriptions, many of which I found too vile to read, but those that I did read... I still recall them now.

And that fiend, that five-pointed star of sin and evil, that vile, unholy abomination, it had been given a name and a title and a brief description which I found so repulsive that upon reading it, I dropped the tome.

The creature was named Kazzkhan and given the unholy title of "Songbird of Lucifer's Will". This was a Demonic mouthpiece of Satan, an unholy abomination which had taken on this hideous, mutated form after falling from Heaven as an Angel cast out in sin.

And the description... upon reading these words, I found myself overwhelmed by disgust and dropped that satanic grimoire.

"Our holy god who has given us insight and wisdom and counsel. He who shall walk among us again and be crowned head of our holy church. He who shall sit upon a great throne above the bishops and the abbots and the cardinals. Kazzkhan shall be our king and our god and our pope and all the world shall proclaim our devout love for him and worship at his feet."

Even now, as I write that, I am uncomfortable. To draw such a thing, to name it... that is one thing... but to claim it is holy, to call it god, to fall down and worship it and to profess love for such a thing... I cannot begin to contemplate the dark, empty depths of depravity and sin to which one must descend in order to view such an inferior, unholy, pitiful fiend as a god.

I dropped that book, feeling deep within my stomach a vile bitterness, a sense like death and rot and mould building within me and I wanted nothing more than to vomit, such was my discomfort and my disgrace for even reading such words.

My attention was quite suddenly stolen by Sister Myrtle and I was given no chance to even think about what I had just read before she began to chant and cry out and pray aloud to the very same cursed abomination which I had just seen depicted, drawn in black ink and red blood.

"Kazzkhan, I call out to you, your humble servant and devoted worshipper!" Sister Myrtle cried out.

She was knelt on the ground now, down on her knees with some sort of curved sacrificial dagger held tightly in her hands which were raised up before her as if in praise.

On the floor in front of her was a bowl filled with herbs and chemicals and...

I realised suddenly what I was witnessing.

This was the night of 16th May 1947, the night Sister Myrtle completed the ritual and summoned the Demon from Hell.

The ingredients for the ritual, which I had read in the burnt remains of her notes... thyme, basil, ginger, garlic and sage... thick, clotted blood... some white, milky fluid... and small, bloodstained bones...

The herbs... a woman's period blood... the semen of a virgin man... and the bones of a stillborn wolf cub.

And there, lying still on the floor beside the wooden bowl of ingredients and chemicals, swaddled in a blanket, fast asleep and sucking their thumb... was a baby.

I wanted to scream and to pick up the baby and drag them far away from the insane nun... but I knew this was a memory of what had already come to pass.

I warned you at the start of this book that this was an uncomfortable, unsettling story and now I warn you again. The things I witnessed...

I have never before shared with anybody what I saw that night. This is the very reason that I chose to write this book, this is the trauma for which this action is therapy.

I urge you... what lies ahead is despairing and evil and cruel and there is no shame in choosing innocent ignorance when it comes to these bleak matters. I tell this story to benefit my own healing, but in no way do you need to read it. What I am about to share... it is upsetting and if you may find yourself in a place of vulnerability in such things, read no further.

For that night, I witnessed Sister Myrtle pray to Kazzkhan. I witnessed her pronounce her love to it, and I watched her commit an atrocious sin to summon it.

"Kazzkhan, my master, my lover, my king! I am your humble slave! My flesh is flesh with which you may do as your please, my heart is yours to consume and my soul is one with your holy being. My master Kazzkhan who art in Hell, harrowed be thy name... I call to you from this sinful, murky, toxic Earth and beg of your love and your mercy. Come to me, my love, come to us. For twelve long centuries we have worked for you, doing your bidding since you were cast out by the Church of false prophets and pious soothsayers who claimed you were sinful. Now, after so long, my love, I have reconstructed the book which you gave us, your loyal slaves, and with it I call to you. Come to me, my love, Kazzkhan, come to me!" Myrtle called out into the night, almost singing the words as though they were an unholy hymn, singing them with giddy glee like a schoolchild who had found her mother's wine rack.

Sister Myrtle then stripped off her habit and knelt down in shameful nudity, the dagger still held out before her, and desecrated the holy sanctity of her own flesh and body, carving into her skin a downward facing pentagram, one which resembled the diagram of Kazzkhan I had seen in the loathsome grimoire. With her own blood still dripping from the dagger, she plunged the blade deep into the bowl of herbs and ingredients and called out once more to her Demonic master "Kazzkhan, I summon you, I conjure you, I call to you, my lover, my slave-master, oh god of my soul, enter me, penetrate me, be one with me!"

The wooden bowl and its contents immediately erupted into flames which burned a bright and violent red and purple and black, yet gave no smoke. Myrtle screamed with delight as I watched on in horror.

She set down the knife and unwrapped the innocent infant from their blankets and held the child over the flames.

"I praise you and bring before you a gift, a vessel, an innocent child who has done no wrong and in your name I dedicate this imperfect soul to you! Let the flesh of the child be your own and may you walk among us through this infant as we walk upon this Earth, my god, come to me!"

79

Sister Myrtle prayed a final time and suddenly the entire room shook. Overhead, thunder shook the building as the ground began to tremble as though there were an earthquake beneath our feet. The tables and desks jumped around and the glass vials and potion bottles fell from their surfaces and down to the floor, where they shattered, exploding into dozens of tiny, wickedly sharp pieces.

The fire began to rise up, transforming into a column of black and red flames which devoured the baby as I screamed in horror and grief.

Suddenly, the ground fell still and the thunder overhead stopped. The flames disappeared and the baby re-emerged, unharmed.

The baby seemed to have an intelligence now, and Sister Myrtle set them down on the ground, only for the baby – a new-born – to stand up straight, entirely unaided. The baby looked down, examining their hands and feet and their body, and looked back up at Myrtle, an unsettling grin spread across their face.

"My god," Myrtle proclaimed, falling down before the infant in perverted worship.

The horrors I witnessed next I shall never be able to forget, no matter how hard I have spent the last seventy years trying.

"Arise," the baby instructed, speaking with a voice that seemed to be so many different things at once. A man, a woman, a goat, a snake, a feral growl and a hungry hiss...

Sister Myrtle did as she was told and the infant began to rise off the ground, levitating in the air such that they and she were at eye level.

No... not the baby. Kazzkhan.

Kazzkhan came forth and began to kiss the satanic nun who had so foolishly summoned that Demon into our world, a passionate, intimate, perverted kiss which made my very skin crawl at the sight of.

But then... then it became apparent that whatever Myrtle had done... she had done it wrong.

Kazzkhan suddenly fell down to the ground and cried out, roaring and bellowing in pain like an angry, cornered beast.

Cracks, bright orange cracks glowing like fire, began to arc and fracture across the possessed child's skin, crawling across the Demon's vessel as it shouted and hissed and roared in pain and agony, swearing and cursing Myrtle, profaning to God such diabolical insults that my ears wanted to close as I heard what the vile Demon had to say.

Myrtle was crying tears of sorrow and pity, seeming to blame herself for whatever was going on, and joined Kazzkhan in cursing herself and cursing God. She fell down and wept at the Demon's feet as the baby began to burn, smoke pouring from their body as the Demon inside wailed in fury and...

Chief Inspector Ryan Godrick had certainly gotten one thing right when stating the events which I now had bore witness to. There had indeed been an explosion in Sister Myrtle's laboratory.

The infant exploded like a firework, sending immolated flaming chunks of meaty gore in every direction and spattering Myrtle's naked, shameful body in the blood of an innocent baby.

And from deep within the core of that deflagrating child, a malevolence burned. The red and black flames exploded forth, seemingly not needing fuel to burn but simply devouring the air as, within seconds, they filled the room and began to pump the laboratory full of black smoke thicker than syrup.

The red and black flames were replaced by normal orange ones and within moments the entire room was ablaze. I tried to get out, my skin blistering from the heat as I choked on the smoke, but a wall of flames stood between myself and the door. Sister Myrtle, covered in blood and stark naked, stood up as I turned around, desperately searching for another exit, which I knew did not exist.

81

The unholy nun stared at me, and I knew then that I was no longer interacting with a memory, but facing Kazzkhan itself.

"Come and fight me, little bitch," the voice of Kazzkhan growled from within the body of Sister Myrtle, and the flames suddenly exploded all around me, sending me flying into a world of darkness. I landed roughly, awakening with a start.

I sat up, taking a moment to gather my thoughts as I struggled to separate my waking mind from that horrific nightmare to which the Demon had just subjected to me. I caught my breath and looked around my room and...

Wait...

No...

This wasn't my room...

The world around me was dark. Overhead, I saw black clouds that choked the sky in darkness, and down below... the amber lights of Ashton on the shore of the inky waters of the loch...

And behind me...

Nestled amongst the forest...

St. Agnes Convent.

Never before in my life had I sleep-walked, but I suppose that didn't matter. The dream had been a distraction. Kazzkhan had shown me something it knew I wouldn't be able to look away from. It had shown me its summoning, fully aware that I would not fight to wake up so long as I bore witness to something which I foolishly thought might give me an advantage on the Demon.

And the fiend had been completely right.

And while it distracted me with sleep and with a nightmare it knew I would stay to watch in the hopes of learning some secret that might prove advantageous... it had led my slumbering body away from the inn and up to the ruins of the convent, alone in the night.

I had not been possessed. I had simply been fooled; manipulated and played like a fiddle.

I climbed to my feet, and stood there.

I was alone, unarmed and unprepared. I had only one crucifix and one rosary on my person and no books of demonology or scripture, no passages to cite, not even a Bible.

I could have turned, I suppose, and returned to the village, but I had read every volume in that inn room too many times to count. I had learned everything I could.

As I said at the beginning of this tale, my brain was ready. I knew the theory, I knew the words, I knew the literature and the lore.

There was nothing left for any book to teach me, nothing left to learn from research or reading or sitting in a breezy little room above a bar and thinking.

All I could do was pray my heart and soul were ready. All I could do was pray that my understandings of the literature would not interfere with my blinding lack of experience.

"God, be with me as I walk now in the company of devils. Let your shining grace fall upon me and may the wisdom of Heaven be with me as I protect the people of Ashton, your children, from this evil. In the name of Jesus Christ I pray," I said aloud, barely able to string a series of words together as my teeth chattered from both the icy cold and from fear. "Amen."

I was alone, I was unprepared, I was in nothing but a habit in the freezing cold and blind in the satanic night without Archie's lantern.

But I was also not alone.

I was with God. The Holy Spirit was within me and the light and love of God filled my veins.

Neither was I unprepared, for God's grace was with me and the holy scripture was within my mind.

Neither was I blind in the darkness, for I walked in faith, and I knew God would not lead me astray.

Kazzkhan had told me to come and fight it.

I stood up straight, and raised my head high. I crossed myself and announced my presence to the Demon.

"In the name of God our Father, in the name of Jesus Christ the Son and in the name of the Holy Spirit, I come before you now, Sister Eleanor Jesse of the Vatican City under the request of Pope Venerable Pius XII and under the jurisdiction of God the Almighty, most high one above all things. I command you, impure spirit, reveal yourself to me!" I proclaimed aloud, calling out to the ruined convent.

The ground began to tremble and a malevolent voice, the same abominable noise I had heard the Demon speak with before, cackled loudly from within the ruins.

I took a deep breath and made one final prayer.

"God...," I began, in truth too overwhelmed by fear to say much. "Be with me. Please."

With that, I stepped forward and though my heart exploded with fear and terror and dread, I strode purposefully and with holy determination into those ruins.

Chapter 6: The Exorcism

I strode forth into those ruins as a knight strides onto the battlefield, for I knew well that a battle is what lay ahead of me. Not one fought with swords or spears or guns, but one fought with words and will and wisdom. I was a knight of God and occupying those ruins was a force of the enemy; a Demon.

I strode forth and immediately felt as though I had stepped foot in a spiritual marsh. The world around me seemed dark and murky, and the air seemed to thicken and slow me down, as though a great and forceful wind blew back against me, except the air was still.

Thunder clapped overhead, but still there was no lightning, and though I heard the wind howling outside the ruins of the convent, the air within was motionless, and not a single branch seemed to sway in the night-time gales.

My footsteps echoed on the stone floors as I strode through the halls of the convent, and I suddenly felt that the entire place seemed much, much larger than it had been before and indeed far more eerie than I recalled. The penumbras gloom seemed to deepen as every shadow seemed to coalesce and broil just in the corner of my eye, as though some mystical forces worked dark spells in secrecy, in corners into which I could not gaze by way of the darkness.

"My God, I pray to you. Be with me and let your grace and mercy shine down upon this place," I called aloud, my tiny voice filling the grim halls of the ruins. Suddenly I felt rather like a fly, caught in a web. Kazzkhan, the spider, was coming.

"Amen," I concluded, before closing my eyes, taking a deep breath, and readying myself.

And so... stood alone without holy water or a Bible or a book of rites, facing against an overwhelmingly powerful Demonic entity who had already, as I have mentioned several times before, murdered seven priests, each with decades more experience than I had at that time... so began my first exorcism.

"In the name of the Father, and of the Son, and of the Holy Spirit," I began, crossing myself, and without pause began reciting prayers from memory, according to the teachings of the process of exorcism which Father Martin had shown me.

"Our Father, who art in Heaven, hallowed be thy name. Thy kingdom come, thy will be done, on Earth, as it is in Heaven. Give us this day our daily bread and forgive us our trespasses as we forgive those who trespass against us; and lead us not into temptation, but deliver us from evil," I spoke The Lord's Prayer aloud, my voice still small, but the hard echoes which came back to me from within those malevolent halls somehow seemed to serve the purpose of making *me* seem larger, rather than giving the impression that I was even smaller; a fly in a web.

Thunder rumbled overhead and finally the wind picked up inside the convent and began to howl and moan through the ruined, roofless halls as, high up above me, the black sky seemed to thicken and darken and gather up itself into a denser, blacker mass, manifesting the abstract of oblivion into the real world above those ruins. I could only assume this was in response to my words and the opening of the exorcism.

"Vade retro Satana!" I called out, literally instructing the Demon to step back, to fall away from this place. Thunder rumbled again, high above, and the ground began to shake. "Hail Mary, full of grace, the Lord is with thee. Blessed art thou among women, and blessed is the fruit of thy womb, Jesus. Holy Mary, Mother of God, pray for us sinners now, and at the hour of our death."

I inhaled, ready to recite a new prayer of honour to the Almighty, but before I could get another word out, the ruins of the convent were filled by the echoing cackles of Kazzkhan, its voice overflowing from the air.

The little fly's wriggling had finally attracted the spider's full attention.

"Vade retro Satana!" I commanded again.

This time, the thunder that boomed overhead was finally accompanied by lightning and the terrible flash illuminated the ruins, for a brief instant, as though it were the middle of the day. Every buttress, every spire, every archway and empty, cold window frame, every charred pew, every stone column and every gothic vault beneath the incinerated ceiling... in the white flash of the lightning, each cast a shadow and silhouette which seemed to sneer at me, a crooked, leering face which snarled down in the darkness.

At last, I saw the eyes which had watched me in the dark.

"Angel of God, my guardian dear, to whom God's love commits me here, ever this day, be at my side, to light and guard, rule and guide," I prayed aloud to the Angels of our Lord the most high God, praying for protection and aid in my battle against the Demon.

Kazzkhan laughed aloud again, a crooked sort of laugh, like a sinful merchant cackling in mirth at a successful scam.

"St. Michael the Archangel, defend us in battle. Be our defence against the wickedness and snares of the Devil. May God rebuke him, we humbly pray, and do thou, oh Prince of the Heavenly hosts, by the power of God, thrust into Hell Satan, and all the evil spirits, who prowl-," I began, but before I could finish my prayer to the Archangel of Heaven's warriors I found myself unable to speak, a hand at my throat with a vice-like grip, the same pink and black, raw and charred hand which had summoned me to the memory of Kazzkhan's conjuring in my dreams.

"...who prowl about the world seeking...," I continued, struggling for breath as I fell down to my knees.

"...seeking... the ruin of... souls," I managed to conclude, before finally running out of breath as I felt the thickening of the air move about me and the presence of the fiendish entity seemed to gather itself up and began to manifest before me.

From here onwards for some time... even now I cannot say for certain about many of the things I saw whether in truth I witnessed real things, or whether

87

what I witnessed was an illusion put in my mind by that Demon. Some things, like the blood rains and the crimson lightning, I knew were real because the townspeople of Ashton saw them too. Others, like the fractured sky and the clouds of burning Hellfire I know now were but illusion... but other things... I still could not say.

For example, I could not say with certainty whether Kazzkhan truly did manifest before me or whether the Demon weaved illusion, but... either way...

Stood before me, Kazzkhan appeared as a thin, malnourished, diseased sort of figure, with skin that was arranged in patches of raw, exposed pink flesh and thick, black, crispy charred regions.

Its eyes were entirely white, like the apparition of Sister Myrtle's eyes, completely milky and pale without iris or pupils, and, as in the picture of the Demon I had seen depicted in the grimoire in Sister Myrtle's laboratory, two black horns like those of a ram had violently burst forth from within the fiend's skull, horns which still dripped with blood.

Kazzkhan had no nose, instead just two nostrils like on a skull, and its mouth was crammed full of long, thin, sharp fangs like those of a serpent, but covering every available space within the cavity of its mouth.

Black, burned wings like those of a bat but each the size of a horse sprung forth from either shoulder of the Demon, and foot-long talons sprouted from each fingertip.

Kazzkhan lifted me from the floor, gripping my throat tight enough to choke me in the powerful grip of its gnarled, twisted talons.

The Demon spoke to me then, its voice as I had heard it before, but now somehow... more real. A man, a woman, a goat and a snake. Two Human voices growling and bleating and hissing together with others, all somehow making a single sound but one which was dissonant and seemed to form discord with creation itself.

"I'll eat your soul, little nun," the vile Demon taunted me, its voice different now, harder even. Not just an eerie echo in an empty ruin or the memory of an evil cackle, no, Kazzkhan now stood before me and laughed in my face.

"Vade retro Satana!" I struggled to choke out the words, commanding the Demon again to fall back as I lifted up my hand weakly and dangled my crucifix in Kazzkhan's face.

The Demon immediately unleashed a roar, a sound which was like an angry goat, a raging bull, a vicious viper and a hateful man all shouting and exclaiming in fury at once as it dropped me to the ground and seemed to melt away into the shadows, still roaring and hissing and bleating as the hateful voice filled the ruins.

I lay there on the floor in a crumpled heap for a moment and struggled to breath, gasping for air and I think I must have been quite purple by now, with bulging eyes and a swollen face as I choked and gasped and slowly clambered up to my feet.

I rubbed my throat, but after a few seconds the shock began to wear off and I somehow knew that I had not yet been inflicted with any permanent damage.

I closed my eyes, clasped my hands in prayer, and fell down to my knees as I continued with the exorcism, determined not to let the Demon defeat me.

"My God, I am sorry for my sins with all my heart. In choosing to do wrong and failing to do good, I have sinned against you whom I should love above all things. I firmly intend, with your help, to do penance, to sin no more, and to avoid whatever leads me to sin. Our Saviour Jesus Christ suffered and died for us. In his name, my God have mercy," I prayed aloud, not even taking a moment to pause before I began a new prayer. "My soul proclaims the greatness of the Lord, holding hands in prayer my spirit rejoices in God my Saviour for he has looked with favour on his lowly servant. From this day all generations will call me blessed: the Almighty has done great things for me, and holy is his name."

89

As I recited the Magnificat, praising our lord God, the convent shook again and overhead the sky was live with dancing sparks of white as lightning and thunder shook the ruins. "He has mercy on those who fear him in every generation. He has shown the strength of his arm, he has scattered the proud in their conceit."

Kazzkhan roared and screamed, calling out profanities and raging insults and blasphemies as thunder and storms shook the ruins and I felt the rage of the entity fill the halls of that dark ruin.

"He has cast down the mighty from their thrones, and has lifted up the lowly. He has filled the hungry with good things, and the rich he has sent away empty," I continued, determined not to let the Demonic tantrum disrupt my flow as I recited the rites to the exorcism, praising God in the face of evil. "He has come to the help of his servant Israel for he remembered his promise of mercy, the promise he made to our fathers, to Abraham and his children forever."

Kazzkhan hissed and roared at me, enraged by my praise to the Almighty while the Demon cowered away in its unholy ruins.

"Kazzkhan, foul snake of Hell and servant of Lucifer, the lowest being in all creation, I condemn you from these ruins and cast you out! You are not welcome nor wanted in this place. You, Demon, who has sullied your divinity with sin and made yourself less in the name of darkness, you are to leave this place forevermore. I deny you this building as a conduit, I deny you my mortal flesh or any other as a vessel and I deny you any right to inhabit this Earth. In the name of Jesus Christ the Messiah, the holy son of the most high God, I command you, oh Songbird of Lucifer's Will, begone from this place," I instructed, my words now seeming to fill the halls with an echoing crescendo of praise to God and damnation to those who oppose him.

There was silence.

The air was still. Above, the black sky was still and quiet, no thunder and no lightning.

All I could hear now was my own breathing and the echoes of my voice receding into silence.

For a moment, I thought I had succeeded. Somehow, I had cast out the Demon where seven other Exorcists had failed.

I clambered to my feet and dusted off my knees, took a deep breath, closed my eyes, and tried to calm my mind.

Suddenly, for the first time since I had entered the convent the previous night, I felt alone. No longer did it seem to me that eyes watched me from every recess in the darkness.

I stepped forth, my footsteps echoing through the halls, but no longer did the sound seem eerie, just... empty.

I strode along the halls of the convent, but I felt no presence with me. I felt no spirit or entity accompanying me in the darkness, I only felt solitude.

I wandered into the cloisters, now just strolling through the ruins, exploring them, and rounded the corner into the courtyard at the cloisters' centre...

Stood before me in a loose half-ring were seven men, each of them perhaps twice my age at the time, in their fifties or sixties. Their throats were cut and their wrists had been slit and the stains of great volumes of dried blood were caked about their chests and arms.

The men were standing before me naked, with inverted crosses carved into their flesh, each constructed from two crooked, jagged gashes deep through their skin, around which more dried blood had accumulated.

They were also clearly dead. Their flesh was pale and bloodless, their eyes were cloudy and their hair had all come out. Each was in a slightly different stage of decomposition, though I suspect the processes of death had been somewhat slowed in each corpse by the Demon, for if these men were – as I suspected – the seven missing priests, then most of them should have been little more than skeletons.

91

All of a sudden, in the same instant that I first laid eyes on the dead priests – at which point I stopped in my tracks in the archway out of the cloisters – I felt the presence spring up all around me, like a whale leaping from the water beneath me, its great maw wide open, only for its jaws to snap shut about me and drag me back into the murky depths of its lair.

Eyes now watched me once more from every angle, staring at me, and in the distance... I saw shapes moving and crawling and squirming across the walls and the spires of the convent, as though strange creatures, too small and distant to see properly, slithered across the ruins.

I turned about by instinct, and behind me was the corpse of Sister Myrtle, the same dead nun I had witnessed in her laboratory in the crypts the previous night. Her eyes, as before, were blind and purely white, sightless orbs. Her mouth was spread wide into a twisted, unnatural, malevolent grimace, and her body seemed all sort of... crooked. It was as though she had gone stiff in lots of places, and the entity that puppeted her had been forced to hold her up in a number of awkward positions to convince her corpse to stand in a perverted mimicry of the Human form.

When the dead nun spoke, the seven priests spoke, all of them in unison, speaking together in the same voice; Kazzkhan's voice. And when Kazzkhan spoke, all of the strange, indistinct creatures crawling upon the ruins of the convent hissed and clicked and cackled together too.

"Pathetic little girl," Kazzkhan hissed maliciously and all of a sudden I felt like such a fool!

All of this came to pass in a matter of seconds and it wasn't until after the Demon spoke that my mind managed to catch up and realised I'd been caught in a trap. The Demon had only pretended to be driven out, only pretended to disappear in my exorcism, and now it had me surrounded. Surely I had weakened it, but rather than staying to fight and defend the ruins, it had slunk away of its own accord, hiding in the corpses of my predecessors, waiting for my guard to be let down.

Once begun, an exorcism cannot be halted. One way or another, it *must* be concluded.

I opened my mouth to speak, about to continue with the exorcism, about to attempt to cast the Demon out once more, but the seven dead priests, moving faster than I could have predicted, rushed upon me and grabbed me, holding me still and putting cold, rotten hands over my mouth.

I wanted to scream, but I couldn't speak, couldn't even move. The naked priests with their slit throats and cut wrists and their inverted crosses, they held me out spread-eagled, two of them on each leg and one on each arm and the seventh with one hand across my chest and the other across my mouth. The stench from his putrid, spoiled hand filled my nose and I didn't even want to breathe that way, I was choking! I struggled to break free, but the Demon-possessed corpses held me tight and I was so sure then that if they wanted to, they could have ripped me apart.

Suddenly, something fell down from above and thudded into the ground beside me. Then another thing... then another... and another.

Whatever those things were that crawled over the building, they were hurling themselves down to the ground, hurling themselves from dozens of feet in the air.

I looked down at them, my muffled screams held in by the priests, as I saw what they were.

Vaguely humanoid, with malnourished, malformed disfigurements – stubby limbs and misshaped heads and crooked, bony spines and... and...

Umbilical cords.

Umbilical cords that hung down from their bellies and dragged through the dirt as these creatures slithered and crawled across the yard or swung through the air as they hurtled down from above.

Infants...

Babies...

Foetuses...

The dead foetuses, miscarried from the poor women of Ashton.

The children that the village never got to meet.

The children that the Demon had killed before they even got the chance to be born, claiming their souls for its own, now manifested into these dark, satanic ruins, these poor children slithered towards me now, crawling through the dirt.

Dozens of them.

They screamed and wailed and cackled and clicked and made noises that a baby might make, noises a goat might make, noises a snake might make, noises that any of them might make and noises that none of them could ever make. They were abhorrent, disgraceful beings as they came grotesquely crawling towards me, their limbs too stubby and too deformed to properly move as they dragged their pale, slimy wet bodies through the dirt, leaving trails of sticky amniotic fluid behind them like snails.

Then one of them climbed onto my foot.

Then another followed.

And another.

And another.

And another.

They began to climb up my legs and crawl into my habit and over my clothes and soon a dozen of them were on me, crawling over my limbs and my body, slithering over my flesh under my clothes and I couldn't help but scream and squirm and cry as I realised I was not ready.

Father Martin was right.

This case... this was a death sentence.

I had been sent here to die.

I had been sent here by the Church to die.

Not because they hated me, not because they didn't like me or thought it was what I deserved.

They had sent me here because I was a woman and because I had no real value to them.

They had, I knew then as I was sure I was about to die, sent me here simply because they were tired of sending priests and losing good men.

Sister Myrtle's dead body came forward, holding one of the dead foetuses in her arms, and stood before me as dozens of the horrifying spirits crawled over my flesh and under my clothes and many more slithered over the ground.

"You're mine now, little girl," Kazzkhan hissed, the dead nun and priests speaking together in the Demon's foul voice as the babies wailed and cried and hissed and bleated. "God is not here any longer. This is my house now. And you're my guest of dishonour."

The priest then, finally, removed his hand from my mouth and I took a deep breath of fresh air, permitted a single moment of respite, before the dead nun came forward and took my chin in her hand, lifting my head back and holding my mouth wide open as she leaned forwards, opening her own mouth and...

I couldn't move, I couldn't do anything, I was utterly trapped, utterly pinned in place, completely within the Demon's control as it forced Sister Myrtle's corpse to open her own mouth wide, mere inches from mine and...

A torrent came forth from her mouth; black ink and red blood and yellow bile and vomit filled with maggots and centipedes and the mashed up bones of dead mice. She was sick into my mouth and I screamed and choked and gagged and cried as the ink and blood and maggots and vomit and bile and bugs spattered violently onto my tongue and my teeth and down my throat.

The priests let me go and stepped back as I fell to the ground and heaved and gagged and choked into the grass, but I couldn't force the Demon's foul toxins out of my body, I was trapped with the fiend *inside* of me.

I knew I was going to die.

I resigned myself to it.

The Demon was inside me, and now it knew me. It knew my mind and my heart and my soul and all at once, I felt the Demon force its way through my very being and possess every part of myself.

It saw the secrets I held which even I did not yet know.

And it could use any one of them against me.

I fell down and lay in the grass as my mind exploded into an inferno of screaming voices and pain as my world became a fiery hot migraine and my very being was ablaze with screaming pain and anger.

I was overwhelmed with a million emotions at once and yet I was numb to the world, choking in vomit and bugs.

I could feel the maggots crawling around inside of me as the voices of the Demon screamed in my ears and I heard nothing else.

"Kill yourself!" the Demon screamed in my ears so loudly that I thought I would go deaf.

"Choke yourself and curse your God who has abandoned you!" it roared.

"Cut yourself and spit in God's face. Slit your useless throat. You are nothing but a gnat and nobody cares. The Church sent you here to die. Your Pope and your God didn't send you here to get rid of me. They sent you here to feed me," Kazzkhan screamed.

"Die!"

"Kill yourself!"

"End your stupid little life!"

"Stupid bitch!"

"Useless wench!"

"Disgrace of a nun!"

"Queer!"

"You will never be loved, not even by God!"

"Your parents sent you away so they could die in peace without you!"

"Father Martin never cared. He sent you here to die!"

"Bitch!"

"Queer!"

"Queer!"

"Shameful little secrets!"

"False nun!"

"Liar!"

"Shameful Catholic little girl!"

"Lesbian!"

"Invert!"

"Homo!"

"Queer!"

"How are you better than a sodomite?"

"Stupid little false nun!"

"You bring disgrace and shame upon your Church!"

"Stupid little queer bitch!"

These words, these thoughts, these screaming lines of bullying came flowing into my ears from the Demon's voice within my mind as I lay there in the dirt in the courtyard of the cloisters.

I cried and screamed and begged for death, I prayed then to God to kill me and send me to Hell.

Because the Demon was right.

It was something I had known, deep down, for many years, and since I had joined the Church knew there was something wrong with me, in those days such things being considered disgraceful and disgusting.

It was an uncomfortable part of myself, something I had hidden away deep in my heart, shielded even from my own mind as I could not bear to witness the truth of my own soul, a truth which I had been taught all my life was shameful and indecent and an unnatural fault, a perversion that made me evil, that made my very soul a mistake...

The Demon, that evil, twisted, malevolent entity, Kazzkhan forced me then to look at myself and everything I perceived as a flaw and told me that I was not good enough.

Because it was right.

The Demon was right.

I was, and am, a lesbian.

And in those days... that meant I was less than Human.

Chapter 7: The Songbird of Lucifer's Will

I lay there, alone in the grass, weeping and crying.

I'm not sure when, but at some point the corpses of Sister Myrtle and the seven priests and the phantoms of all those dead foetuses left me, abandoning me to Demonic solitude in the dirt.

I was possessed.

Though I have been inhabited by Demonic forces many, many times since 1951, this was the first time I ever acted as a vessel to a Demonic entity, and it is not something I have ever found easier.

My head felt overcrowded, as though rather than simply containing my own soul, my mind now played host to thousands of people, all talking and arguing and screaming inside my skull. My lungs felt like I had spent a century smoking a pack of cigarettes every day, and my hands and feet were rife with pins and needles as though the blood to them had simply stopped. My chest burned and my stomach felt like it was about to stage a revolution, except I was denied the ability to throw up, like a hand gripped my oesophagus tightly from within my own flesh.

Every single part of me felt sick and disgusting and violated, as the Demon forced itself inside every part of my body. I could feel it slithering and squirming around inside my chest, in my thighs, in my throat, in my groin...

I had often in past wondered why it was called a "possession" and asked where that word had come from.

Now, finally, I understood.

I had become that Demon's property. I had become an object which it owned; its possession.

"Stand up, you filthy little queer whore," the Demon commanded me as a thousand satanic voices screamed in my mind and though I tried to fight it, the only way to make them stop was to obey.

99

I stood up.

"Go down to the conjuring chamber; Sister Myrtle's laboratory," the Demon then instructed and the voices screamed and howled at me, growing louder and louder and angrier and angrier, hurling abuse and insults and slurs and terrible, horrifying words inside my mind until I had no option but to crawl into a hole and let myself wither away and die, or do as I was told.

I took a step forward.

Then another step.

And another.

And another.

And another.

I had no choice.

The Demon was not grabbing my arms and manoeuvring me itself, but I still had no more choice in my actions than if it had been.

I left the courtyard behind and then followed the cloisters around, stumbling about like a drunk as the spirits of the Demon inside me toyed with my legs for its own amusement, sending me tripping and falling about as I attempted to navigate my way to the stairs down into the crypts.

As I stumbled along, I passed the main doorway in and out of the ruins, and I stopped.

I could leave. I could deny the Demon of whatever perverted games it wanted to play with me and I could just leave.

It would scream and shout and hurl abuse at me all the way but...

The loch...

I stumbled along into the archway and gazed out onto the scene at the foot of the hill; the little amber lanterns of Ashton twinkling in the fog and the great, inky black shores of Loch Ashie.

In the dark, the waters looked just like a hole, a great, big, black hole into nothing. Like a gateway down into Hell itself.

Some small part of my mind which still could think clearly made that connection and an idea, fully formed, sprang forth in my mind.

I could go to the loch. I could take the Demon far away from the convent and drown myself in the loch.

Kazzkhan wanted me to kill myself, that much had been apparent since the moment its spirits entered my body, but it wanted me to do it in the convent, presumably as part of some sort of Demonic ritual. I could only theorise that possessing the priests and forcing them to commit suicide in the same way had been part of some sort of black magic incantation to cause the miscarriages in the village, presumably so that Kazzkhan could claim the innocent souls of those sinless infants for itself.

But what if I denied the Demon its ritual?

What if I denied it my body out in the loch, far from the convent and the other corpses it had accumulated? Left without a vessel or a conduit to cling to, the Demon would have nowhere left in this world to go. Nowhere but down...

I could banish Kazzkhan back to Hell.

But, if I drowned myself in the lake... I knew I risked damning myself to Hell as well. Suicide is a mortal sin, though I do believe that the wisdom and love of God makes exceptions in circumstances such as these, for I would be sacrificing myself to save the town, not just committing myself to a meaningless death. Regardless, I knew I risked Hell, but if sending Kazzkhan back to Hell and saving Ashton from its evil meant taking the Demon back down there myself... then I was more than willing pay the price.

101

I stepped forward, out through that archway, and began to stumble and struggle against the pull of the Demon as it fought me and tried to force me back toward the convent, hurling abuse into my soul, cursing me and swearing at me, calling me such abhorrent things that even if I could remember the Demon's exact words now, I don't think I would want to recall them here.

I think if I could recall and transcribe every terrible curse and sinful word that entity called me then, I could write a whole other book just on its creative and abusive use of profanity.

"I will suck on your soul," the Demon raged in my ear. "I will kill you myself. I will use your fingernails to slit open your own stomach and spill your intestines on the floor, then I will make you eat them!"

For the first time, I dared to respond to the Demon. "You will be silent and go back to Hell!"

If I had thought it was angry before... my retaliation rendered the Demon completely engulfed in rage.

I felt a physical force grab my arms and legs then, as though unseen hands made from the wind gripped my flesh tight, with talons that dug into my skin. I saw the blood that those claws drew from my veins, but I fought on.

I steeled my determination and kept going, though I still cried out.

The entire experience was utterly surreal and in truth I could not tell you now how much of it was real and how much was illusion.

Certainly I was a mess. I was scared and alone and undergoing a terrible, torturous bullying while every part of my body ached and spiked and hurt in a different way to each other part of my body, and my mind burned with black Hellfire.

Yet simultaneously I was determined. I think my entire character, my entire soul, had been temporarily stripped of all identity and personality and Humanity and distilled down to a single trait, one individual character-defining sensation and at last I understood why each of the seven priests had failed.

When possessed by the Demon and distilled down to a single sensation, I did not become a force of rage or fear or bargaining or depression or hatred, as many quite understandably might and which, in those seconds I knew, the priests must have become.

Instead, I was defined by stubbornness.

I was an immoveable object, and Kazzkhan just was not quite an unstoppable force.

I mean to bring no shame upon the memories of those seven priests. I am sure they were good men, but when possessed and broken past the limits of sanity, I think whatever they became left them wanting. Whatever features of their identity emerged under such insane circumstances... they were not the priests' best features at all.

That is not to claim either that my stubbornness is my best feature.

It was, however, exactly what I needed at the time.

For my stubbornness and my determination kept me moving.

As Kazzkhan's invisible claws tore into the flesh of my arms and legs, I kept fighting, I kept moving forwards, I kept dragging my broken self away from those ruins.

I distanced myself from Kazzkhan's nest and from the dark chambers housed within the grim crypt beneath.

I prised myself away from Sister Myrtle's sacrificial blade and tore myself from the dark fate of my seven priestly predecessors.

"Stop fighting, you stupid, insolent little queer," the Demon cursed me savagely. I could hear the spit flying from its black lips within my mind.

"This is my body," I responded through gritted teeth. "I am in command, not you."

"I OWN YOU, YOU STUPID GIRL!" it roared and suddenly I think its rage surpassed a certain point.

I felt a great and terrible force seize me, as though I had been struck by an enormous train, and I was lifted a dozen feet into the air and flung backwards all the way through the convent arch and to the heart of the ruins, to the foot of the altar. Above me, an upside-down stone statue of Jesus Christ was nailed to an inverted wooden cross; yet another act of sacrilege and blasphemy which this dark entity had committed in the name of the darkness.

What I saw next...

The nightmare to which I now bore witness... I am certain that this was but an illusion which the Demon span within my mind and yet... I do not think it was any less real. This was some sort of manifestation of the war in my mind between the Demonic force of Kazzkhan and my own mortal soul.

Firstly, the walls of the convent exploded and fell down, and melted away into shadows in a moment, leaving me lying alone on a barren hilltop, with black skies above me and the black waters of Loch Ashie below.

Then, high above me, a great bolt of lightning cracked its way across the sky, except this was no momentary flash, but a seemingly permanent new feature in the black dome overhead. The orange and red fiery jagged arc splintered through the black clouds like a fracture in the sky itself, and deep from within, the voice of Kazzkhan bellowed unholy words in a language I did not recognise.

The crack began to widen, stretching out into an enormous, jagged disc of red, orange and black flames and smoke, something I recognised from my vision of the night of Kazzkhan's summoning; Hellfire.

That disc of fire in the sky... it was a gateway to Hell itself.

And from within...

Kazzkhan emerged.

What I saw... this was no depiction in a book, nor a feeble manifestation of the Demon in this physical world... I saw the huge and terrifying faces of the Demon. I saw Kazzkhan's true form; an entity more visceral and obscene and offensive to the eye than I had ever imagined. Even if I had ever doubted it, I knew with certainty this could have been no dream, for until I had witnessed such things, I lacked the imagination to conjure up those images of my own accord.

Firstly... Kazzkhan's body vaguely resembled the trunk of a man, with great muscles across its chest and broad shoulders, but its skin was burned black to ash and charcoal, with enormous sections of its body savagely shredded apart as though by being mangled in some sort of machinery, with massive sections of gristle and bones visible beneath raw and ruined flesh.

Two such bodies existed, one beside the other, and they joined at the waist, giving the Demon a single pelvis with two hips, and a single belly button, but two chests and four shoulders. From the vile monstrosity's perspective, its left side was a man, while its right was a woman, and each was as hideously burned as the other.

Its flesh was black as charcoal, with raw pink muscles and sinews visible beneath the cracks of its burned skin. Each face was hideously scarred, with jagged rips through their cheeks that spread their dauntingly unsettling grimaces from ear to ear. Within their open, eerie mouths were rows upon rows upon rows of teeth, each far longer than a tooth has any right to be, and each as wickedly sharp as the fangs of a serpent. Red, blood-soaked forked tongues flitted about inside each head's mouth, and they both had completely white, blind eyes, devoid of irises or pupils.

Its four ears were pointed and elven, but had been ripped and mashed savagely. From within its two skulls, ram horns had violently erupted, and black, oily blood still dripped from the horns.

Its arms were unnaturally long, all twisted and bent in strange ways, as though they had been broken in dozens of different places, and each finger ended in an enormous, black, wickedly sharp talon.

The lower half of the Demon, joining to the waist of the two-bodied monstrosity above, was largely constructed from the hind legs of a black goat, with the red and black tail of a serpent emerging from its shaggy hind.

All over its body, the Demon had been tattooed and mutilated with thousands of occult symbols and strange characters, some of which I recognised from ancient, forbidden texts kept within vaults beneath the Vatican, others which I had only seen in Sister Myrtle's cultic grimoire; The Book of Kazzkhan.

This enormous fiend which now descended from above, coming down from the Hellish gateway, was easily as colossal as the hill atop which I lay, and from behind its back the fiend spread four singularly immense wings, each like the blackened and burnt wings of a dragon or an enormous bat, with torn and charred webs of leathery flesh and sinew stretched thin between colossal, skeletal talons.

Gathered all about this Demonic figure was a raging thunderstorm which seemed to be part of its being, as though the sheer existence of the fiend had summoned the storm to reality.

I noticed that the Demon wore a huge belt of leather and rope and twine, and hanging down from the belt were thousands of ropes...

No...

Not just ropes...

Nooses...

From seven of them hung the seven priests, from one of them was Sister Myrtle, and from dozens and dozens more...

The foetuses of the miscarried children of Ashton...

The souls of the dead whom Kazzkhan had claimed for its own.

And now... stood before me... glowering down from on high... was the true nightmarish form of the evil, satanic entity which was possessing me.

I knew even then that this was all in my own head, and that what I saw was nothing but illusion, and yet within my mind this was the truth. The Demon loomed over me as a monolithic statue of oppression and Hellish oblivion, a gargantuan beast of raw hatred and overwhelming sin, abuse and desolation.

"Weep before my grandeur, queer bitch," the Demon roared, its voice louder now, not deeper just... bigger. "I'm going to make you kill yourself, you stupid little queer, and I will devour your soul."

I was pinned down, paralysed within my own mind, able to think but not to speak or move or do anything.

Kazzkhan's two crooked, twisted faces widened their grotesquely mutilated grins and the fiendish entity began to cackle again. "Perhaps I have gone about this the wrong way... perhaps a more... personal approach would be appropriate."

The ground beneath me, just dirt and ash in place of the convent ruins, began to squirm and writhe as thousands upon millions of tiny... things... began to emerge. Flies, maggots, spiders, insects... perhaps smaller things that were simply the spores of fungi... began to emerge from the ground and swarm around me, crawling over me and around me and covering me up until my vision turned black and...

And then, by some act of spiritual contortion, Kazzkhan somehow forced my living consciousness into my own memories as I was gifted with an illusion from the Demon.

A dream which I had before lived out.

A nightmare.

A memory I had forgotten...

I awoke slowly and groggily, my head uncomfortable and heavy and my body feeling awkward and weak, and I was quite frustrated I think, trying to work out what on Earth had awoken me at such a ridiculous time.

I was fifteen years old, in September 1939. I had been in the Church for a few months now, a novice initiate preparing for a life of servitude to the Lord, but still very much new to all these things.

At the time, I and half a dozen other girls of a similar age bunked together in a small room off the chapel of the convent in which we were being trained, and to this day I have no recollection of what that place was called. I remember though the names of the girls I bunked with. There was of course myself, known then just as Ellie, not Sister Eleanor, Mary, Agatha, Margaret, Christine, Deirdre and Meredith. There was an eighth bed in the room, but as long as I stayed there it was cold, empty and unoccupied, a silent corner in the room and the one part of our little chamber which seemed resilient to the warm mirth of our collective burgeoning friendships.

I was close with all six of the other girls and by now I knew them all quite well. Deirdre had been brought over from Ireland just before the war began, Margaret had been there for almost a year and was originally from London. Agatha and Christine were twin sisters from Birmingham, the youngest of our group at thirteen and had in fact only arrived a week or so prior. Meredith, a sixteen-year-old, was the oldest of our group and I think both I and Mary rather looked up to her, for she was all that we aspired to be; devout, humble and wholesome in every way.

Mary Chester, however... Mary was the girl in that troupe with whom I was the closest. We had both arrived around the same time and had grown terribly close as we both accustomed ourselves to life in a convent. Mary was a few months my senior, and in fact would be turning sixteen within a few weeks, while I had only been fifteen for around four months. We each spent more time with the other than with any of the other girls and it was scarce to see one of us devoid of the other though the nuns who trained us certainly tried to keep us separate whenever possible.

Now... as I was disturbed from my sleep on that uncomfortable bed, I saw a familiar face grinning down at me mischievously as Mary gently shook me awake, her long blonde hair tickling my nose as it hung down over her ear.

She was a soft, gentle sort of girl really, but she had a wicked sense of humour and a crooked streak about her, always ready for shenanigans and hijinks if the opportunities so arose.

In truth, I was rather infatuated by her I think. She was certainly my closest friend at the time and loitering in her presence almost guaranteed that I should find boredom to be a rarity. And now, as I lay in bed, slowly clambering from my peaceful slumber to a state of reasonable consciousness, I felt my heart accelerate as I predicted the oncoming mischief which Mary's waking of me was sure to guarantee.

"Get up," she tenderly whispered in my ear and gleefully slunk away to wait for me by the door. Within moments I had scrambled hastily but silently from my sheets and thrown a coat about my shoulders as I prepared to disappear with my best friend into the night, dressed in nothing but a thin jacket and my nightie, though the September air was bound to be pleasant enough and I certainly didn't anticipate finding myself in a state of chill, lest the wind be particularly fierce.

Together, the pair of us silently slipped out into the halls of the convent, walking barefoot to keep our steps muffled and robbed of echoes. I couldn't help but giggle in stifled laughter as we, carefree and unburdened as children are, slunk from the convent and out, into the open night air. The sky was black but the moon and stars were bright and gifted us generously with light enough to see our ways about in the dark. In fact, the moon's light was so intense that our silhouettes cast harsh shadows upon the ground as though sunlight rained down from above, though I admit our shadows were far fainter than they might have been in the daytime.

I was so young then.

So innocent.

Just fifteen years old, living in a world at war, far from parents who I had not heard from in weeks… and yet none of that weighed upon my mind as I shared joy with Mary. In those precious moments we were innocent, we were just children, we were free of expectations or commitments or the stresses of life.

We ran out into the dark and frolicked merrily on the slopes of the hill and watched the dark clouds drift lazily from one horizon to the other while the moonlight gave us sight to see one another in the blue and grey darkness of God's Earth.

We chased one another about, playing tick – Jules has told me to correct myself and call that game tag, but I grew up in Liverpool and I will call that game what I like! – and laughing quite gayly all the time. At last, exhausted, we both collapsed down in the grass and pushed and jostled with one another playfully, affectionately.

Back then… I didn't even know who I was really. I didn't know what love was, I barely understood the concept of affection, we were so young and the young are so free of such knowledges.

"Won't it be so dreadful when we're all old and wrinkly like Mother Superior?" Mary joked to me. The Mother Superior of our convent must have been in her late fifties at the time, certainly not young, but as I sit here at ninety-seven I can't help but laugh at what a poor concept we had of how *young* we were.

I just laughed back at her, but I soon realised that though she had been joking, in truth she meant what she said as she looked up to the sky and seemed to gaze in introspective wonder.

"I mean it," she added thoughtfully. "We're so young now. So beautiful. Won't it be such a tragedy for us to be old and shrivelled?"

I shrugged, not really sure what to say. Mary always came out with the oddest things and I never learned to predict what she might say next.

"They're all just... stood still," she complained, continuing after an unresponsive moment from me. "They've gotten older and older, all those nuns, but they haven't once changed since they were our age. They're all pure and clean and holy and... and just so... so boring. Where's the fun in that? Who wants a life like that with no fun? A life of just... boring... Who wants it? I don't. I didn't ask to be brought here. I just got sent here like you did. I know you didn't ask for this either."

I didn't say anything for a moment longer, but thought about what she'd said.

"No, but...," I began, struggling to put my thoughts to words. "What adult has fun at all? I have rarely ever seen my mother smile, and only my father when he fakes it. What grown-up is happy? At least the nuns here have purpose."

Mary seemed surprised by that comment.

"You *want* to be a nun?" she asked, as though the very thought of it had never even occurred to her.

I realised then just how apathetic she was to it all and... I confess my adolescent need to fit in overpowered my faith in that moment. I was just a silly child.

"Of course not," I lied and immediately felt a wave of shame wash through my soul. "I mean... I'm just saying... they haven't chosen a worse life than anybody else... doesn't mean I want it though."

Each new word was like the twist of a guilty knife in my heart as I knew full well that my words were false, but I couldn't stop myself from deceiving her. I wanted her to be my friend so much... I felt a dependency upon her for it.

Mary leaned in towards me as we lay there on the grass, coming closer to me.

"What *do* you want then?" she asked.

111

I opened and closed my mouth several times as I tried to think of an answer.

I wanted to be a nun.

I wanted to devote my life and soul to Jesus Christ until the day I died. I was in love with the Church and in love with God's majestic creation and I wanted nothing more than to serve as God's missionary upon the Earth.

What could I possibly say?

"I don't know," I shrugged eventually, failing to feign being casual.

"Me neither," Mary shrugged in return. "I want to do whatever I want though and never answer to a nun or a man and especially never to God. I want my life to be my own."

I just nodded and shrugged again, rather trapped in a realm of awkward indecisiveness as I lied to her and tried so desperately to hide myself away behind a façade which I hoped she might find more acceptable.

Mary shuffled closer again and locked eyes with me.

She had terribly bright green eyes. Startlingly green, green like the most luscious grass caught in the midsummer sun. Her eyes almost seemed to glow with personality as her crooked streak, her mischievous streak, shone through those bright green eyes and warmed my heart.

"Can I tell you something?" Mary asked me quite abruptly. "You have to promise not to tell a soul."

She added the second line very suddenly, as though it were all something that overwhelmed her inside her head, but which she found ever so difficult to manifest from within her mind into the real world.

"Of course," I told her tenderly, always ready for anything she might say, though never predicting what that may be.

She nervously bit her lip a moment, before vigorously shaking her head and looking away. "No... never mind."

My heart sank and I think I must have pouted. "Oh... no, please, tell me."

She looked back at me and I think I really must have been pouting because she seemed to melt inside when she turned back and saw my face.

"Oh, Ellie...," she crooned softly, seemingly on a knife edge between two uncertainties.

"Very well, but...," she seemed to give in eventually. "Just..."

She kept starting and stopping, pausing and beginning a new sentence with a new word, only to give up and seemingly found whatever she wanted to say entirely impossible to get out past her lips.

"I just... I think... I know... I... I...," she kept on for a few moments before shutting her mouth altogether, apparently incapable now of speech at all.

"Oh for goodness' sake," she exclaimed eventually. Before, she had been so incapable to convict to a single decision that she simply bounced from uncertainty to uncertainty but now...

Without warning, surprising me and I think surprising herself, Mary leaned forwards all of a sudden and...

She kissed me.

I am ninety-seven now, and I have only ever been kissed twice in my life. Once as a child in 1939, and the other in 1985, almost fifty years later. I am hardly a connoisseur in such matters, but each kiss stirred within me a deeply different reaction. If pressed to summarise how I felt about that first kiss in 1939 in a single word, I think the word I might choose would be 'afraid'.

I lay there a moment, in the grass, staring in shock and disbelief, struggling greatly to comprehend what had just happened.

We were meant to be nuns. We were learning to devote our lives to God. And Mary had just kissed me. I found it all a confusion and a contradicting absurdity, the very idea of her, a novice nun, kissing me, another novice nun. It wasn't until a few moments later that the homosexual component of the

113

kiss dawned upon me and then I was filled with shame and confusion and an overwhelming feeling of disgust and guilt and... so many more emotions that as a mere fifteen-year-old I was ill-equipped to comprehend what I felt at all.

I lay there a moment and stared at her, as Mary's expression of shy joy rapidly faded into one of concern, then anxiety, then fear and panic as I think she realised that I was not in the slightest bit prepared to process how I felt about what had transpired. I think she had observed my homosexuality in the previous months, but I think only now did she realise that even I was oblivious to it, and certainly I was not ready to discover it yet.

"Ellie, I... I'm so sorry... I thought... it was just a joke... sorry... forget about it... please... please forget about it...," she stammered as blind panic seemed to fill her mind.

I was still rather in a state of shock, and without really thinking or feeling or making conscious choices, I sat upright, climbed to my feet, and returned to the convent, to our room off the chapel, and to my bed, walking alone in complete silence. I lay there for a while, incapable of sleep, and thought restlessly about what had happened, but no matter how hard I tried to convince myself of my feelings on the matter one way or the other, I found I had no choice but to accept that I had enjoyed it. I had enjoyed kissing Mary. And that made me deeply afraid.

I liked her. I liked her more than the other girls, but I also liked her differently than the other girls. She was special to me for some reason and I began to wonder if that was what love was, if I was broken because I was feeling love for a girl instead of a boy, if perhaps I was better off as a nun and choosing to love nobody but God...

I lay there for ages.

After an hour, Mary returned, with red eyes like she'd been crying, and slunk back into her own bed without acknowledging me, as though the thought of even seeing my face again after that was too much for the poor girl to bear.

I lay there for at least another few hours before exhaustion set in and my mind fell away into sleep.

The next morning, Mary refused to meet my gaze at every opportunity, throughout the day, she didn't dare even glance in my direction. Over the coming week, we didn't speak once to one another and the nuns seemed to finally feel as though they had successfully kept us apart themselves.

I thought long and hard for a week about what had happened, and at last I made up my mind about what to do.

I had been told that such things were sins and marks of Satan. Then there was only one thing to do. If truly I was to be a devout servant of God, then I had to thwart the enemy at every turn.

I thought perhaps God was giving me a test, and I thought that the decision to betray my friend would be one which would lead to my passing the test. I thought that if I followed the rules I would be righteous.

I acted out of fear, not compassion or love or kindness. What I did to Mary... a loveless, cruel act of a frightened child and for eighty-two years I have carried with me that terrible guilt.

One week after the midnight incident, I went to Mother Superior and I told her what happened. I was honest with her about sneaking out, I confessed the sins of my lies to her, and I told her what Mary had done. Mother Superior heard my confession and told me to wait in the dormitory off the chapel until she had decided what to do about it.

I sat there, alone, for hours, before at last another nun came in to take me to Mother Superior.

"Eleanor, I have thought and prayed carefully about what you've told me and I have reached a decision. You did the right thing in telling me about this. False vows and liars are not easily forgiven and you have saved young Mary from a life of such things. Homosexuality... this is the mark of an evil soul, and in divulging this information with me, you have helped us find evil in our convent and remove it as one removes a weed; by the roots," Mother Superior told me sternly, but kindly. "The weed, Mary, will be dismissed from our cloister at once. I am sure the guilt you have carried this past week has been enough of a burden upon your young mind. The penance for your lies to Mary is the shame you hold within you for those sins, no further punishment will be necessary. You have done well, Eleanor. You will make a great nun someday, I know it!"

With that, I was dismissed.

That night, there were two empty beds in our room. As were there two empty beds the night after, and the night after, and the night after...

Mary was gone. She had been dismissed and sent away, I never knew where to.

I never saw her again.

Such an intimate friendship, shattered in a single night by the impatience of her infatuation and the fear of my repressed attractions.

And, I confess, by the cowardice of my own disloyal and unloving actions.

For the rest of my time in that place, the following five years, I was subject to a chamber of six girls and two cold, empty, soulless beds. Two cold corners to keep our joy at bay.

And for me... those beds were a constant reminder of the cowardice of my actions against Mary, and of the secret affections hidden in my heart.

Because... I enjoyed that kiss... and I had been as attracted to her as she had been to myself. And with that knowledge came shame. Thick, black shame which I wrapped about my heart like a blanket. Shame so thick, I had forgotten what was inside it.

I had forgotten Mary, I had forgotten that friendship, I had forgotten my affections. I had forgotten it all.

For twelve long years.

Until 1951.

Until I was possessed by Kazzkhan.

"You broke her heart and got her sent away," Kazzkhan whispered in my ear. "You ruined her. Why? You weren't loving, you weren't kind or Godly, you weren't being a holy little saint, were you? You were being a coward. You were being selfish and afraid and cruel. If I didn't know any better, I'd say you would make a pretty good little Demon. Except you're too much a stupid little girl to be a Demon."

I wanted to cry.

I lay there on the barren hill as the monolithic figure of Kazzkhan loomed above me, a great silhouette engulfed in black smoke and thunderclouds. A sentient storm like a dead god, reigning above me beneath a gateway of Hellfire.

"You're a treacherous little queer, aren't you? Is that how you treat everybody you fall in love with? You go and tell your other nuns and your priests and your bishops and you get them in trouble? Is that how you show love? Torture and cruelty and ridicule? You'd make an excellent Demon," Kazzkhan laughed to itself, a deep and hearty snicker which seemed to make the ground tremble.

As the Demon laughed, red lightning, crimson like blood, began to rumble and flash across the sky as it began to rain, but not with water... it rained blood.

Blood fell down onto my face and soaked into my now filthy habit as the Demon laughed and laughed and laughed and the abuse and cursing and profanity and blasphemy continued to echo through my head as the voice of the Demon insisted that I get up, I climb down into the crypts, I find Sister Myrtle's sacrificial blade, and I kill myself.

Once more, I found the overwhelming strength and rage of Kazzkhan overpowered me and washed over me so forcefully that my whole being and my entire identity were diminished down to a single thought, a single concept, a single sensation.

Before, I had been nothing but a stubborn force of determination, but now… now I was a cold being of calculation.

I was numb and devoid of feeling, instead I found my soul free of a heart and instead rendered a boundless mind, and my mind flew into action.

Thoughts and ideas and theories exploded and danced and chased one another inside my mind as disparate notions and concepts all swam together and all of a sudden fell into my lap as a plan.

The Demon could not control me. It needed me to make the decision, it needed me to make my own choices, it had no power against my freewill, it could only influence me.

It wanted me to kill myself in a ritualistic manner such that it could use my death in a black magic curse of witchcraft to slaughter every unborn child in Ashton and reap their souls. That was Kazzkhan's goal, and it would take any means necessary to reach that goal.

But it remained my decision whether or not the Demon was successful.

This was my mind, my heart, my body and my soul.

I was in command.

Kazzkhan was bigger and older and smarter and more deceptive, but I had all the power and all the authority.

It was time I used it.

At last, I understood how exorcism works.

Authority, skill, and the union of the two.

An exorcism cannot be done simply by declaring words to a Demon and praying it will go away. Our prayers have power and authority, but without understanding or conviction that power is wasted. We must direct that power, we must be driven, we must use that power to our advantage.

Swinging a sword will do no help if one does not know how to thrust properly, how to block and parry, how to feign and, crucially, how to dance. A swordfight is a waltz with a winner and an exorcism is a swordfight with prayers versus curses.

In my first exorcism, I simply lunged and stabbed at the Demon wildly with my words, inexperienced enough to not appreciate the purpose of my actions, while it tricked me and frightened me and spun illusions to distract me until I was possessed. Had I not been fortunate in possessing the virtue of determination, I would have been forced to commit suicide by the Demon and another wave of unborn souls would have been harvested from the village below.

Now I understood.

I was familiar before with the concept of blocking and parrying and such, but now I appreciated the necessity of their use.

Now I knew I could fight back.

It was time now for a rematch.

And I had an advantage which I had not possessed before, and one which the seven priests before me had never had the chance to gain.

I had the advantage of having fought Kazzkhan before. I had lost, but in doing so I had gained experience of this specific Demon. I had seen its tricks, seen its moves. I knew its fighting style well.

Now I could counter it.

Chapter 8: A Final Attempt

I stood.

Groggily and wholly uncertain of the potential for my continued survival, but faithful now in the result of my conviction against the enemy, I stood.

Somehow, despite the overwhelming rage and power which swarmed around me and held me down, despite the fury of the Demon which had wormed its way into every inch of my mind and dug sharp hooks deep into the tissues of my flesh and of my brain, I stood.

I closed my eyes and crossed myself and began my exorcism anew. "Glory be to the Father, and to the Son, and to the Holy Spirit. As it was in the beginning, is now, and ever shall be, world without end."

"You stupid little girl!" Kazzkhan laughed, a deep, roaring laugh. That was its first attack. "You thick little queer, you have already failed!"

It was trying to kick me while I was down, trying to remove my hope by reminding me I already had failed, and so the Act of Hope prayer would be my reply.

"My God, relying on thy infinite goodness and promises, I hope to obtain pardon of my sins, the help of thy grace and life everlasting, through the merits of Jesus Christ, my Lord and Redeemer," I prayed aloud, and in doing so declared the very hope which Kazzkhan sought to revoke.

"It won't work, you are too weak, you are alone, you stupid failure," Kazzkhan taunted from high above me.

But I was not alone. And so I prayed first to my Guardian Angel and then to St. Michael the Archangel.

"Angel of God, my guardian dear, to whom God's love commits me here, ever this day, be at my side, to light and guard, rule and guide," I began my first prayer, before continuing with the second. "And St. Michael the Archangel, defend us in battle. Be our defence against the wickedness and snares of the

Devil. May God rebuke him, we humbly pray, and do thou, oh Prince of the Heavenly hosts, by the power of God, thrust into Hell Satan, and all the evil spirits, who prowl about the world seeking the ruin of souls."

Kazzkhan seemed to finally crack a little, for the first time the power of its being seemed not to be enough as it recognised my retaliatory attacks against its cruelty. "I will kill you, do you understand me, you stupid little invert?"

Kazzkhan's curse meant to belittle me, it meant to remind me of my insignificance and that I was at its mercy, and so my reply was the Act of Faith prayer, for while I am small, the God whom I worship is mighty and faith in such divinity gave me strength and authority against the adversary.

"Oh my God, I firmly believe that thou art one God, in three divine persons, the Father, the Son and the Holy Ghost; I believe that thy divine Son became man and died for our sins and that he will come to judge the living and the dead. I believe these and all the truths which the holy Catholic Church teaches, because thou hast revealed them, who canst neither deceive nor be deceived," I prayed aloud, before a thought occurred to me and I added an additional line to the rite, one specifically against the Demon itself. "And I believe thy judgment, oh my God, shall fall righteously upon your sullied creation, the Songbird of Lucifer's Will. I believe and know to be true that thou art a good God and that the Demon shall not stand in thy light."

Kazzkhan actually hissed now, and the Earth beneath me began to tremble as the Demon hissed and spat in rage.

I was beating it.

"Damn you, queer little girl. I am Kazzkhan, I am a god! I am the divine mouthpiece of Lucifer, Empress of Hell. I am the lieutenant of Belphegor, King of Pride, and your small words cannot overthrow me!" Kazzkhan boasted, roaring with blasphemy as its words of Demonic praise filled the air and I knew that my response had to counteract its self-praise. And so, I gave praise instead to God, balancing its proud blasphemy with selfless adoration of the Almighty.

121

"Glory be to the Father, and to the Son, and to the Holy Spirit. As it was in the beginning, is now, and ever shall be, world without end," I praised, before continuing with the Magnificat. "My soul proclaims the greatness of the Lord, holding hands in prayer my spirit rejoices in God my Saviour for he has looked with favour on his lowly servant. From this day all generations will call me blessed: the Almighty has done great things for me, and holy is his name. He has mercy on those who fear him in every generation. He has shown the strength of his arm, he has scattered the proud in their conceit. He has cast down the mighty from their thrones, and has lifted up the lowly. He has filled the hungry with good things, and the rich he has sent away empty. He has come to the help of his servant Israel for he remembered his promise of mercy, the promise he made to our fathers, to Abraham and his children forever."

Kazzkhan roared and bellowed and hissed and cursed me again and again and again as I worked, but no matter its attempts to distract me, I ignored it and moved on. Snakes slithered up in my habit as I knelt on the ground, and wrapped themselves around my thighs under my clothes. Insects came and swarmed about me as bees and gnats and wasps stung my arms and my neck. Terrible pain came upon my stomach as I felt as though the most abhorrent cramp of my entire life seized every strand of muscle through my abdomen, but no matter how the Demon tortured me, I refused to give in.

The Demon resorted to screaming abuse and bullying inside my mind once more, a thousand voices telling me to kill myself, to cut myself, to profane in the name of God, to curse my creator, to beg for death, and as the pain and fear and despair seized my heart, I refused to give in to the hatred of Kazzkhan. Instead, I recited the Act of Love prayer, "O my God, I love thee above all things with my whole heart and soul, because thou art all good and worthy of all love. I love my neighbour as myself for love of thee. I forgive all who have injured me, and I ask pardon for all whom I have injured."

"Give in!" Kazzkhan roared in my ears. "Just give in, you stupid girl. Are those rude mortals worth your suffering? Is the Chief Constable down in that village worth your suffering? You do not know them! They are strangers, how can you sacrifice your life for them? Why do you endure such pain?"

"I love my neighbour as myself for love of thee. I forgive all who have injured me, and I ask pardon for all whom I have injured," I repeated, answering the Demon's rhetorical question with praise of the love of God.

"They will not thank you for your troubles!" Kazzkhan told me cruelly. "They will still hate you. Even if it is not *you* they will hate. Queers and inverts and lesbians, you will never be loved. You will always be feared and hated. If they knew who you were, if they knew *what* you were... they would stone you to death you sinful, shameful little girl."

I held back tears as Kazzkhan's words stung my soul.

Because I believed him.

The world hated people like me. We were not Human, we were less...

"No!" I defiantly told myself as I realised I had let Kazzkhan get the upper hand on me. "No more!"

I had had enough of this vile spawn of Hell telling me who and what I was.

"I have enough personal demons to deal with telling me what I am, oh Songbird of Lucifer's Will. I revoke from you the right to join them!" I roared back, my single voice just as loud as the Demon's thousand. "My God, I am sorry for my sins with all my heart. In choosing to do wrong and failing to do good, I have sinned against you whom I should love above all things. I firmly intend, with your help, to do penance, to sin no more, and to avoid whatever leads me to sin. Our Saviour Jesus Christ suffered and died for us. In his name. My God have mercy."

"Your God will not help you!" Kazzkhan shouted at me so loudly, so offensively that I felt the very Earth crack beneath my feet as the angry Demon threw a tantrum at its inability to control me.

"God already is help me!" I shouted back, my voice just as powerful. "This is my mind, Demon, and you are *not* wanted and you are *not* welcome here. You are a worshipper of the lowest of all the beings of God's creation and so you are a fool and a heretic and an imbecile. I condemn you back to Hell and I command you now to leave this vessel, to vacate my body. In the name of the Lord God our Father, in the name of Jesus Christ the Son, the Messiah of Nazareth, and in the name of the Holy Spirit whose being flows through my soul, I command you Demon, begone! Vade retro Satana!"

Kazzkhan screamed and shouted and hissed and bleated, and I heard then the voices of seven men and a woman mixed with the cries of the Demon and the whimpers of a thousand infants as Kazzkhan raged at the power of my faith and the weakness of its pride.

I stood now and for the first time since I had renewed my exorcism, I opened my eyes and faced the Demon.

The illusion of the absent convent and the Hellfire portal in the sky had been banished now and Kazzkhan stood before me, in the same two-bodied form but now the height of any Human.

"I revoke from you your right to my flesh. I revoke your claim upon the souls of the unborn infants you have stolen, upon the souls of the seven priests whom you murdered, and upon the soul of Sister Myrtle whom you tricked and deceived. I revoke from you their souls and release them into the loving hands of God's merciful judgement, while you, Kazzkhan, spawn of Hell and Songbird of Lucifer's Will...," I began, pausing for breath and I think smiling with confidence as Kazzkhan seemed to be injured by each point, by each instruction until it knelt down on the floor before me.

I stepped forwards and knelt before the Demon, gripping its ribbed ram horns and lifting its two heads. "Get out of my body. Get out of these ruins. And get off of this Earth."

Kazzkhan screamed and hissed and bore its hungry fangs at me, but it seemed now powerless against my devotion and faith.

124

"Go back to Hell, you pathetic worm."

Suddenly, the manifestation of the Demon dissipated into nothingness and at last I felt within me a terrible churning as I vomited all over the floor of the ruins, knelt down beside the altar of the convent.

Blood, ink, vomit, maggots, bugs and mouse bones came from my mouth as I emptied my stomach there onto the floor. Every time I thought I had stopped, I began to heave and gag again as my body fought ferociously to purge my being of the Demon's foul contagion and its spoilt toxins were eradicated from my stomach. I must have heaved and thrown up at least twelve or thirteen times over half an hour before finally my body was at peace with itself.

Never in my life have I smoked, but I imagine that the sensation of coughing up a wad of tar from inside one's lungs is not dissimilar to what I experienced then. Afterwards, my mouth tasted like I had been chewing on dry ashes and leaves.

I fell down then and leaned against the altar. Somehow, I knew I had not quite won yet, however.

The Demon had left my body, yes, but I still felt furious eyes glare at me from the shadows.

I may have momentarily won the battle, but an exorcism is a war.

Round one had gone to the Demon and now round two was mine, but there were more still to come.

The first blatant sign that I was still not alone in the ruins was the earthquake. Once the Demon had been cast out of my body, the ground began ferociously to shake and tremble. The ruins groaned and rumbled and I was sure they would collapse again as small stones and rocks jumped and danced upon the ground as the Earth itself seemed to reverberate with the fury of the Demon.

What could I do but pray? And so pray I did.

"Angel of God, my guardian dear, to whom God's love commits me here. Ever this day, be at my side, to light and guard, rule and guide," I prayed aloud, calling out to the forces of Heaven, summoning them to combat the dark adversary from Hell against whom I was opposed. The earthquake then stopped and the disembodied voice of Kazzkhan groaned and roared from all around me, filling the ruins of the convent.

I looked around and saw shadows crawling and climbing and slithering across the walls, flickering as though the place were illuminated by invisible flames, as though the memory of that terrible fire raged still through the building.

Voices screamed and called to me from the shadows, the voices of women, screaming and crying out, and I knew immediately that I was hearing the screams of the twenty-five nuns who had perished in that fire four years ago. Whether I simply was hearing the memory of their deaths, or whether Kazzkhan now tortured their true souls in retaliation to my exorcism in an attempt to punish me, I could not say. But either way, I heard their screams and saw the flickering light of that dead fire as the ghost of the tragedy still haunted the ruins.

Again, however, I knew all too well that there was nothing I could do but pray.

Kazzkhan offered me the memory of a tragedy, and so in response I instead chose to remember God's love, through the Memorare. "Remember, O most gracious Virgin Mary, that never was it known that anyone who fled to thy protection, implored thy help, or sought thine intercession was left unaided. Inspired by this confidence, I fly unto thee, O Virgin of virgins, my mother; to thee do I come, before thee I stand, sinful and sorrowful. O Mother of the Word Incarnate, despise not my petitions, but in thy mercy hear and answer me."

Again, Kazzkhan roared and hissed from the shadows, growing quieter and weaker now than ever before.

The screaming and wailing of the dying ghosts grew louder now, louder and louder and louder, and the shadows began to burn with such stark contrast between light and dark that the walls themselves seemed to be ignited anew, with a war between two fronts of flame dancing through the ruins; a whirlwind of white flames versus a raging storm of black fire battled through the air, which simmered and broiled in the heat.

"Hail Mary, full of grace, The Lord is with thee. Blessed art thou among women, and blessed is the fruit of thy womb, Jesus. Holy Mary, Mother of God, pray for us sinners now, and at the hour of our death," I prayed, again calling out to the Virgin Mother of Jesus Christ, showing utter devotion to my faith in the face of imminent death as the air filled with the black smoke of Kazzkhan's raging Hellfire.

"Just die already!" Kazzkhan screamed at me, its voice hollow and ragged from so much screaming and shouting.

I was winning, I knew it.

"Our Father, who art in Heaven, hallowed be thy name. Thy kingdom come, thy will be done, on Earth, as it is in Heaven. Give us this day our daily bread and forgive us our trespasses as we forgive those who trespass against us; and lead us not into temptation, but deliver us from evil," I prayed, beginning to draw to a close as I put my foot down in final submission to God and eternal defiance against the adversary.

The fires disappeared, fading into the air as they were revealed as nothing but illusions as Kazzkhan was finally prised from the ruins, separated from its conduit in this world.

I crossed myself one last time as I finished the Demon off. "In the name of the Father, and of the Son, and of the Holy Spirit, I command you, Kazzkhan, go back to Hell."

"Damn you, bitch!" Kazzkhan spat and the ground trembled one last time as ash and soot and dust lightly rained down through the ruins, and I knew then that I was alone in that place.

"Amen," I finished confidently.

127

Kazzkhan was gone.

Its presence was well and truly banished.

It was over.

I had won.

I clambered unsteadily to my feet then, struggling to get up as every part of my body ached with exhaustion and I managed to stumble out to the edge of the entrance arch of the convent.

Kazzkhan had been banished.

At last, after four years of terrorizing that poor town, it was done. No more would their pregnancies be afflicted, no more would their skies be full of thunderclouds without lightning, no more would their animals be plagued with death.

No more were they cursed, held under Demonic oppression.

They were free.

I had freed them.

A so-called suicide case which I was doomed to fail, and I had won.

The Demon was gone and Ashton was free, and as the sun rose in the distant east, illuminating the Loch and the village and the ruins, I saw the great view which St. Agnes Convent offered in daylight for the first time, and it was gorgeous.

Beautiful green hills with lush forests and rolling meadows, and a great, misty loch to the north, and down there, nestled amongst the hills on the southern shores of the mysterious lake, the quaint little village of Ashton.

This was what I had been fighting for.

"In answer to your question," I spoke aloud, though I knew Kazzkhan was gone and could hear me no more, "yes. They *would* have been worth dying for."

I don't really remember much after that, I must admit.

I think I may have passed out, largely from exhaustion and partially from the physical trauma which being possessed and performing an exorcism on one's own self seems to cause, but either way, I don't recall what came next for a while. I was stood there, tiredly leaning against the blackened stone archway at the entrance of the ruins, and soon after, my world was plunged into darkness.

I was not afraid however. I knew my soul was free of the Demon, and I knew that, thanks to me, Ashton was free now too. I had victory. That was all I was concerned with. Gladly would I have died then for Ashton.

Chapter 9: My First Case Closed

I dreamed for a while. The details of it all were rather fuzzy for a time afterwards, but I am certain that I dreamt of my ordeal in the ruins, possessed by Kazzkhan, and recalled the memories which the Demon had used against me.

I stirred some time later, I think it cannot have been more than an hour or two since I finally overthrew the Demon, and I found myself laying there, in the dirt, in the archway which once served as the entrance to the convent. Slowly, my eyes opened as I stirred from my slumber, and as my wits gathered about me, it finally dawned on me how truly lucky I was.

Seven priests had come here before me.

Seven Exorcists each with decades of experience over me.

One by one, each of them had attempted to overthrow Kazzkhan, but all of them had failed, all of them.

But not me.

Where they had failed, somehow, I had succeeded, but not by skill or by knowledge, simply by pure luck.

Luck that had caused my character-defining stubbornness and determination to shine through when the rest of my soul had been cast into the Demon's shadow.

Well, I say luck.

Some might call it luck, those who believe the world is truly dictated by acts of random chance.

I would be tempted not to call it luck, however, but the guiding hand of God. With God's help, the dimness of my inexperience had been irrelevant when compared to the blinding light of my faith in the Almighty.

God had saved me there and then, in those ruins, and as I awoke, that knowledge came into my mind, and I found myself rather comforted by it. God had helped me overthrow the Demon. The words of my prayers would have been hollow; dulled swords, if it were not for the sharpness of God's wrath.

I climbed shakily to my feet, unsteady after my ordeal through the night, and stretched a bit, letting my stiff joints loosen and come more readily free of the aches and pains which my resting hours asleep in those ruins had brought me.

I was shivering too, I suddenly realised, having been oblivious even to the freezing chill up there until that very moment, but of *course* it was cold! It was Inverness, Scotland, in January! I was amazed I hadn't died of hypothermia in my sleep.

I didn't want to move, of course, I wanted to just find somewhere warm in the convent to shelter myself away, but that wouldn't do. I really didn't want to stay in the ruins a moment longer than necessary, so I supposed I had no choice but to get going.

So, I headed off, putting one foot in front of the other and marched as calmly as I could back down the hill, down to Ashton. It took me a little longer than usual to get down there, and it must have been midday by the time I stumbled into the village, covered in dirt and dried blood and with dozens of holes torn into my dishevelled habit, what a sorry sight I must have been!

I stumbled into the village, and as I crossed Ashton and headed towards The Bloody Stallion, everyone I came across met my gaze, smiled to me shyly, and nodded.

They knew.

They all knew.

Of course they knew, this was their village and places like this are notorious for how fast word travels within them. They knew why I was here, they knew where I had gone, and they knew what my return meant. They knew they were truly free.

But they had never even acknowledged their enslavement, so how could they now acknowledge their freedom? So instead they just smiled and nodded, but that was enough. They were free and they knew it, and I didn't care about the rest. I wasn't interested in their praise or their gratitude, only in their peace, and I had returned peace to them.

I smiled back to them and nodded back and that was all, not a word needing to be said, but we both knew. In every interaction with every villager, whomever each one might have been, we both knew.

I entered the inn, stumbling forwards into the dark room, and every eye fell on me. This time, however, their expressions were not looks of judgement or anger, but looks of gratitude, faces filled with calm relief.

I went up to the bar and sat down, across from Archie.

"Is it done?" he asked me quietly. I think he thought it was too good to be true. He must already have heard a dozen rumours, but I had come to know how Archie thought quite well in the last handful of days, and he did not trust his neighbours.

I didn't speak my answer, instead I just nodded to him, smiling tiredly.

Archie's breath caught in his throat as he choked back tears.

"No miscarriages last night. Though we did get a minor earthquake... and it rained blood... but... you really did it, didn't you?" he asked again, still not quite letting himself hope, not letting himself believe me.

I smiled at that news. I think even I hadn't quite believed it, some anxious part of me still feared Kazzkhan was hiding up there in the ruins somewhere. But if it *was* up there... it would not have let me escape. It would not have let me sleep in undisturbed peace. And, more crucially, if Kazzkhan had remained, it would not have ceased its torments on the pregnant women of Ashton.

132

"I did. I exorcised the Demon. Kazzkhan is gone. I sent it back to Hell. It will be a very long time before that Demon comes back," I assured Archie, smiling to him, letting myself relax for the first time since I arrived in the village.

Archie almost broke then, almost. He choked back tears again, and looked across the pub, meeting the gaze of each of his patrons one by one.

"Go home," he told them all. "Go home. Tell your families they are loved. We are free. This is not a day to drink alone in the tavern."

One by one, stools and chairs scraped their legs across the floor and red-faced old men climbed to their feet and slowly ambled out the door. Some of them met my gaze, and smiled, single tears dripping down their cheeks.

Once the room was empty, I turned back to Archie, who by now was almost fully crying, and we smiled to each other.

"I knew you were special, but..." he chuckled through his tears of relief as the last four years of stress and fear finally slid off his shoulders. "You really did it..."

I laughed then. "Yes, I did it. It's okay, Archie, it's over. The Demon is gone. For good."

Archie stood up straight, breathed in deep, and steadied his nerves. "In that case... if you ever want to come back, to visit us, then you'll always have a room here for free, and you will always have food and drink here on the house, in honour of your great service to our village, in honour of your kindness to us."

I smiled then and let myself relax just a little more. "Thank you, Archie, but it was my pleasure to help."

I wasn't quite comfortable being rewarded for my actions.

"Please, it's the least we can do. Now, you must be starving, let me make you something," he told me, and disappeared into the kitchen to start cooking for me.

He brought my food through a bit later and fed me well, and then I went up to my room, packed my things, and returned downstairs, ready to be on my way.

Archie arranged for the same kind boy with the applecart and the donkey to take me back to Inverness, and from there I quickly found myself on the train back to Rome.

It was all a bit of a whirlwind, and I didn't really feel as though I got much of a chance to say goodbye to Archie, who had fast become a close friend, but then again that might just be my memory of that afternoon fading. I was dreadfully tired, absolutely exhausted, and it was all seventy years ago now so forgive me if I have forgotten anything.

I don't believe I ever got a chance to see Chief Constable McIntosh on my way out either, but that was alright. I should certainly have liked to see the look on his face when he realised what I had done for his village, but equally he was a small, afraid man, and though his rudeness to me had been unacceptable, it was still understandable. What retribution might I have received by seeing him again? Only an apology to fuel my own pride, or some confrontation which served to help nobody. It was, I think, for the best then that I never saw McIntosh ever again.

I had helped them, and I knew it. I needed nothing more to put a smile upon my face.

The ride in the cart was in comfortable silence and though the air was cold, the sunlight was bright and fought off the chill quite nicely. The boy thanked me for what I had done for his town, and bid me farewell as I entered the station.

I sat there, at my platform, for a little while, and mused on everything that had happened over the last few days, recalling my own thoughts and experiences, and debated how much information I should disclose when I wrote up my report.

I was not ready to admit to the Church my homosexuality. I would at once be dismissed and everything I had worked for over the last twelve years would immediately have been put to waste. Equally, I was not ready then to admit it to myself, not ready to see myself the way that the Demon had forced me to. It had shown me a side of myself that I was not prepared to bear witness to.

I was not ready for that knowledge, yet it was mine.

I sighed as I sat there, on a bench on my platform, and stared at the railroad tracks ahead of me, down there, over the edge of the platform.

I kept trying to write my report in my head, but the words just kept falling apart. Was it lying to hide my homosexuality? Was it a sin? Was I being sexually immoral just by *being*? By hiding myself from my superiors?

The Church would have said yes. They would have told me I was being sinful for being lesbian, even though I wasn't even *doing* anything, I was just living my life. I hadn't even thought about breaking my vows, I had never been tempted to go against my vows of chastity, yet I knew the Church still would say I was sinning.

So why did I feel it was so unfair?

Why did I feel like I wasn't doing anything wrong, even if they said I was?

No, I had to work this all out within myself before I could share it with the Church. Was it lying to hide it from them? Maybe it was. Maybe it wasn't.

But I wasn't hurting anybody by failing to disclose the intimate violations Kazzkhan had unleashed upon me. I wasn't harming anybody in the Church, or myself, in fact I was protecting myself from harm.

So I wasn't hurting anybody, and I wasn't being selfish. Protecting oneself is not selfish. Loving oneself is not selfish. Avoiding pain is not selfish.

But back then... I wasn't so sure. I thought perhaps I was sinning, and perhaps I was a mistake, and in hiding that I was being selfish. I felt like I was sneaking around, avoiding a well-earned punishment, when in reality I know now I was doing no such thing.

I felt terribly alone and afraid as I sat there in the train station.

I didn't even want to pray about it.

I know, me! I didn't want to pray.

But I was so afraid that I was doing the wrong thing, so afraid that I was mistaken that I was afraid to ask God for help, afraid to ask for advice, because I was so terrified of discovering myself to be an abominable mistake.

I think I must have cried then, as I sat there, alone on my platform in the train station in Inverness. I was exhausted, I was stressed, I still felt violated and unclean after my possession, and as I sat there in my painful solitude, I cried.

My train would be coming soon, of course.

I would get on my train soon and return to the Vatican.

I would have to write a report on all this.

But for now, for that moment, I just sat there, alone, and I cried.

Epilogue by Sister Eleanor Jesse

Well, there you have it.

My first case.

I truly do feel better after sharing that, as though the burden of that dark knowledge is no longer mine alone. The things that Sister Myrtle did, the cruelty and sinful depths of depravity to which she was able to sink... such things have haunted me for seventy years.

Now, I hope I will stop seeing her walking corpse in my dreams.

Some things that may be worth mentioning:

I kept in touch with Archie for a while after these events and though we lost contact in the mid 1970's, I know that he married a sweet girl named Ava in 1957, and together they had two sons – named Rodrick and Fergus – and a daughter named Eleanor. I was honoured when Archie told me his daughter had been named after me, and indeed I met all three children a handful of times in the 1960's, and he was as good a father to them as he had been a friend to me.

Ashton ceased to have any Demonic signs after I dealt with Kazzkhan and to this day has never experienced so much as a clap of thunder in the absence of lightning. The town was, within a decade, quite back to normal, and I am overjoyed by the knowledge that I was able to bring them salvation from that dark fiend.

Throughout this book, some of you may have noticed that I have referred to the Demon, Kazzkhan, only with the pronoun *it*. The pronouns like *she*, *they* and *he* refer to people or living things, such as you or I, or my late beloved cat Cecil, while *it* implies an object. It is solely with the intent of insulting that Demon that I use the pronoun *it*. Kazzkhan is not a living entity or a person. It is a Demon; a vile, dead spirit of hatred and evil and is not worthy of comparison to the Human being by way of personal pronouns.

137

I would also like to offer my assurances that although at the measly age of twenty-six I had not begun to acknowledge my homosexuality, and despite the abuse I faced from the Demon Kazzkhan, I am very comfortable with my identity now and have come to accept myself and all facets of my being as a beautiful creation of God. These events began my journey of self-acceptance, though the fact I eventually came to love myself did nothing to ease the pain which that cruel monster inflicted upon me.

It may also be of interest to share the information that Jules and I managed to accumulate in more recent years thanks to the wonders of the internet. I knew none of this at the time, and this lack of knowledge did not hinder my ability to combat Kazzkhan, but you, as a reader, may still find this interesting.

Friar Geoffrey was a monk who, in 782AD, was possessed by Kazzkhan and murdered the brothers of his monastery and used their skins to create the pages of the Book of Kazzkhan, that bleak grimoire which finally was destroyed by the summoning of that same Demon in 1947. Friar Geoffrey died during the process of exorcising the Demon, at which point the Church seized the grimoire and secluded it in a library of forbidden texts deep beneath Rome. In 1137AD, some 350 years later, the followers of Kazzkhan successfully infiltrated the Church and stole the grimoire, during the process of which the book was damaged and several sections were torn out and lost, including the pages which referred to the exact methods of summoning Kazzkhan back from Hell.

After a further eight centuries of trial and error, the Cult of Kazzkhan, a satanic order within the Church, successfully achieved their ultimate goal when Sister Myrtle finally summoned the Demon.

The conjuring was imperfect however, likely Myrtle was fractionally mistaken in her attempt by an ingredient or two, but the botched conjuring meant that Kazzkhan's Demonic essence was incorrectly concealed within the infant offered up before it by the nun, which led to the poor baby deflagrating, as I witnessed, which then caused the fire which burned down the convent.

Without a vessel – a living mortal host – Kazzkhan was forced to settle for the ruins of the convent itself and the physical corpse of Sister Myrtle for conduits – inanimate objects which serve as hosts of the Demon – to anchor its being to our world, which meant the Demon was stuck in the convent. I can only presume that other branches of the cult were watching from afar and scheming new ways of removing the Demon from the ruins, but I foiled those schemes when I sent the Demon back to Hell.

This was, of course, only the first of many, many hundreds of cases, but I think my lack of experience beforehand and the dark severity which accompanied it, such as the foreboding knowledge of the seven missing priests, meant that this case in particular has always featured quite potently in my mind, even after so many years.

I will see now if indeed writing these events down helps me to rest more easily. After so many years... letting go of these dark memories will come as a relief.

Jules, my oldest friend who I have mentioned several times in this tale, has urged me to publish this book when I complete it, and indeed I may well do so. If indeed this act does prove to help me move on from these traumatic events after so many decades, I think perhaps I will write about another case.

But which to pick? I have seen so many things...

If indeed I write a sequel to this book, I think I shall tell the tale of how Jules and I came to meet. In that case, it would be the case of St. Bernard's Hospital in Louisiana in 1966, the case of Sister Amelia.

But for now...

I have spent all the day writing this book. I have sat here at my desk in my little cottage and I have done nothing but write, and now midnight draws near. The end of the day and the end of the month, for tomorrow is June.

Soon I shall rest, and I think when I awake I will send this manuscript to Jules and see what he thinks of it all. I know he himself has a book which he would like to share with the world, a tale of the dark fiend Vulwarz which he and his students fought a few years ago. I have read the accounts of that book and I think if he should encourage me to publish this then I too shall tell him to publish *that* tale.

We shall see. He can be ever so stubborn.

I suppose what I'm saying is that I don't really know what I might do next. But that doesn't bother me. When you get old you stop worrying about the future because you know you haven't got much of one left to worry about, especially when you're as old as I am. Ninety-seven!

I'd like to get to one hundred. Yes, one hundred would be good and proper. A nice, big, round sort of number to top it all off with. That gives me three years at least left to tell you my stories. I may give myself some time before I start writing again, and certainly I think I will go a bit slower next time... doing all this in one day has rather left me quite exhausted, and at my age being exhausted is no small thing.

I suppose I'm rambling now, aren't I. I've been told I do that, but what can you expect? I'm ninety-seven, as I said, for goodness' sake! I didn't get all this old without wanting to get a good few ramblings in before I croak.

I think I shall finish off this book now by sharing a little wisdom that this case taught me.

Demons are real and terrifying and overwhelmingly dreadful sorts of things, but why should that mean we cannot defeat them? They are dead things, and we are alive. They are dead, like statues or photographs, but we... we are fluid and changing and living. They cannot adapt to the new, while we constantly change and evolve. Thus, we have dominion over them.

So remember, whether the Demons you battle are personal or Hellish, you have one thing that they will never have. You are alive and you are real and there is no greater honour nor greater power than the strength of life and of love.

If you are reading this, I am praying for you. Remember that you are loved and valued more intimately and more completely than any Earthly thing can express and that no matter how dark this Earth gets, *we* are the lights to combat the darkness, the campfires to cast out the cold.

And, I think, that is all I have to say about that.

Live well, and be kind,

Sister Eleanor Jesse.

Afterword by Ebony Jasper Eldritch

Here we find ourselves once more; on the last page.

Another book over, another tale told, and what a joy it has been to tell this one! Sister Eleanor Jesse is rapidly becoming a favourite of the characters I have created and her place in my heart is huge.

I have more stories of Sister Eleanor to tell yet, and indeed the tale of her life has only just begun. She does, after all, have almost a thousand cases to share and while I don't think I'll manage a thousand of these books, not quite at least, I think four will do nicely. A nice little quadrilogy of four books.

The second of these, Sister Amelia, will be released some time in 2022, but I have other projects in the works to keep you entertained before then.

The name of this book was the first thing I came up with, long before any characters or plot came into being. The plot then steadily evolved and the Demon known as Kazzkhan came to appear, while Sister Eleanor's personality emerged from an otherwise unrecognisable protagonist. Once I had a plot and a character, I knew fairly quickly where the rest of the tale would be going, and indeed the lovely Sister Eleanor came to be based on myself, or at least she became based upon who I should like to be (aside from the nun bit).

It took me a few months to write this, though Sister Eleanor claims she wrote it all in a day, but this tale and these characters always took me to places I didn't quite expect to find myself in. Archie, for example, wasn't going to be a major character at all, instead he was intended simply as an expositional barkeep in the fifth or sixth chapter, but as I sat there and wrote chapter two, he suddenly introduced himself and rather threw me off.

This one really does get quite dark in some places, I will confess, and the gory detail into which I have delved is unsettling to say the least, though I have put several warnings throughout, in Sister Eleanor's voice, to ward off the easily disturbed from the more graphic sections.

I already have begun work on the sequel, Sister Amelia, and I'm really looking forward to getting that all down in writing.

Stay spooky,

Ebony Jasper Eldritch.

Printed in Great Britain
by Amazon

75993489R00081